NOBEL
GENES

Also by RUNE MICHAELS

# GENESIS ALPHA
# THE REMINDER

# NOBEL
# GENES

## RUNE MICHAELS

ATHENEUM BOOKS FOR YOUNG READERS
NEW YORK LONDON TORONTO SYDNEY

ATHENEUM BOOKS FOR YOUNG READERS
An imprint of Simon & Schuster Children's Publishing Division
1230 Avenue of the Americas, New York, New York 10020
For information about special discounts for bulk purchases, please contact Simon & Schuster Special Sales at 1-866-506-1949 or business@simonandschuster.com.
The Simon & Schuster Speakers Bureau can bring authors to your live event. For more information or to book an event, contact the Simon & Schuster Speakers Bureau at 1-866-248-3049 or visit our website at www.simonspeakers.com.
Book design by Michael McCartney
The text for this book is set in Berling.
Manufactured in the United States of America
First Edition
10 9 8 7 6 5 4 3 2 1
Library of Congress Cataloging-in-Publication Data
Michaels, Rune.
Nobel genes / Rune Michaels. — 1st ed.
p.  cm.
Summary: A boy whose manic-depressive mother has always told him that his father won a Nobel Prize, spends his time taking care of her and searching for clues to his identity, but eventually he finds his own truth.
ISBN 978-1-4169-1259-0 (hardcover)
[1. Manic-depressive illness—Fiction. 2. Mental illness—Fiction. 3. Identity—Fiction.
4. Single-parent families—Fiction. 5. Emotional problems—Fiction.
6. Family problems—Fiction. 7. Incest—Fiction.] I. Title.
PZ7.M51835No 2010
[Fic]—dc22
2009036665
ISBN 978-1-4424-0717-6 (eBook)

TO THE MEMORY OF MY MOTHER

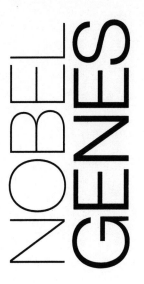

NOBEL GENES

1

I'm a donor baby.

But not just an ordinary donor baby. Mom wanted a genius baby, so she visited a special sperm bank, to buy me genes from a Nobel Prize winner. She wanted to ensure that her child would be a prodigy, someone special, someone who would give to the world something new and wonderful.

Something went wrong. I'm just a regular kid. I'm not a prodigy. Mom can't understand why, why my Nobel genes aren't showing themselves. She says she can't understand why my phenotype doesn't correspond better with my genotype. That sounds really weird, but it means she can't understand why I'm not what I'm supposed to be.

Once I suggested she must have strong genes, stronger than the Nobel genes. I meant it as a compliment, but I guess it wasn't. She laughed, and then she stopped laughing and just looked at me funny, and then she started to cry and wouldn't eat anything that evening.

I've had my IQ tested about a million times, although it's been a while now. Mom keeps hoping I'll start to "blossom," but it hasn't happened yet, and I don't think it ever will. I've learned some of the correct answers on the tests, and I'm getting pretty practiced at the puzzles, but it doesn't help an awful lot. I've never made it into the genius category. I've seen my numbers, and they call it high average. Mom's disappointed. I've seen the way her gaze skims over "high" and settles on "average" and then moves to me; that heavy, sad gaze that makes me feel like I'm something tiny enough to fit under a microscope. Sometimes I think she'd like to take me back to the sperm bank and ask for a refund.

I've wondered if something's wrong with my brain, if I'm only average because something went wrong. Maybe I didn't get enough oxygen to my brain when I was born or something, but because genetically I was meant to be a genius to begin with, I was brought down to normal instead of further down. Sometimes that's almost comforting, to imagine that deep down in my genes I'm as brilliant as my dad is, as brilliant as my mother wants me to be.

Maybe it skips a generation. Maybe my kids will be brilliant and then Mom will finally be happy again—she'll have a genius grandchild.

I'm not going to let my kids know they carry brilliant Nobel genes, and I hope Mom doesn't say anything. I'll just watch silently and if they show promise, I'll help them find the right direction. That's all. It doesn't work, trying to force yourself to become a genius. I've tried that and it's impossible. When I try to understand complicated things, like the relativity theory, it's like trying to get ahold of something while wearing a thick glove.

I do well enough at school, but there are other kids who do just as well. The only class I'm really good at is art, but there's no Nobel Prize for drawing or painting.

Mom wanted me to get a scholarship to a school for the gifted, she wanted that ever since kindergarten, but I never scored high enough on their tests for that. We're not doing that anymore. I'm glad. Mom thinks I'm not trying hard enough, I guess, not applying myself. Sometimes she blames the school, because often gifted children don't do well in school because they're bored, the school isn't challenging enough for them. Sometimes she blames herself for not having sent me to a special preschool for gifted toddlers, to kick-start my gifts and my love of learning, and when I try to comfort her by telling her it wouldn't have made any difference, she gets angry.

A while ago my mom started thinking my Nobel dad might not have been a scientist after all—he could have been a writer, he could have won the literature prize, and if so, my genius would not be in mathematics and physics, it would be in creative writing. She laughed when she realized this, laughed and clasped her hands around my head, saying something about the wrong brain hemisphere.

And for a while she was happy. She sent me to a summer camp where we read literature and wrote short stories and poems. It was the first time I was away from home, ever. It was fun, although I couldn't help worrying about Mom. It was the first time she was alone too, the first time since I was born that she wouldn't have anyone to tuck in at night and check up on five times before morning.

But it was okay. When I went home they sent a big file with me, filled with everything I'd written. Of course, when you've been playing around at writing your thoughts down, you don't want your mom to see it all. It's private—and well, there are a lot of things Mom can't handle, a lot of things that make her problems worse. So I had to do some serious censoring on the bus back home.

I took out everything that had to do with my feelings about my dad, and everything that had to do with my worries about my lack of genius, and also some other private stuff. There was a lot left, all the exercises we'd done, and a lot of silly poetry and what the teacher called "philosophical musings," just general pondering about how the world worked and stuff.

Mom didn't suspect I'd left stuff out. I'm not sure she read it all. She couldn't have had the time. While I was away she'd researched literary agents and had a stack of envelopes ready on the kitchen table, names neatly printed on the front. It must have taken her ages, and she spent the night after I came home going through my folder and putting examples of my work in the envelopes.

The next morning she sent me to the post office with the whole bunch. I thought about throwing them away, but I was afraid she'd somehow find out, so I mailed them all.

Over the next few months the replies dropped in through the mail slot. At first Mom rushed to the door every day when she heard the postman, but then she stopped caring. She left the mail on the dresser by the door for days, sometimes, before ripping the envelopes open with her lips pinched, scanning the few lines, and then tearing the letters up and throwing them into the trash can she kept there for junk mail. I guess I don't write very well.

Whenever she was asleep when the mail arrived, I'd tear up the responses myself to save her the trouble and prevent bad days. That turned out to be a mistake. She had a checklist of all the people she'd contacted, and after a while she started calling those who hadn't replied, even though she hates to talk on the phone. She'd get angry with them sometimes. I wasn't caught, though.

After that, my mother thought my father might have been a Peace Prize winner. You don't have to have any special talents to win the Nobel Peace

Prize, you just need to have done something good for mankind. So you don't have to be a genius in the traditional sense; there's no need to be good at physics or mathematics or even creative writing.

She was really excited about that for a while, and I was glad, because she was happy again, and when she's happy, nothing very scary happens. She got me books on sociology and politics, bought me a huge revolving globe from a catalogue, and signed me up with Amnesty International. She spent days in front of the muted television with a pencil and a pad, occasionally jotting down notes, wondering which minorities we belonged to and how I could fight for our rights.

I wasn't sure how to fight for our rights. I didn't think we were particularly oppressed. I told Mom so, and she got annoyed and said I'd just have to pick a cause. There were plenty to go around. One day she sent me off to the library to research the world's problems and bring home a list of possible causes to fight for.

I found out more than I ever wanted to know about the world's problems. I could go for political prisoners, child slavery, literacy, global warming, saving animals in danger of extinction—there are a million worthy causes to fight for. I was depressed at the end of the day when I closed down the last charity website and stacked my books together, sighing so loudly that the librarian behind me asked if something was wrong. I told her no, but I should have said yes. My list filled several pages in my notebook. There's a lot wrong with this world, and I never knew about it.

When I got home, Mom asked me if I'd chosen a cause, and I said I needed some time to think about it. But before I'd chosen one, she'd again settled on science and enrolled me in an after-school physics program—after all, most Nobel Prizes go to scientists, so the odds are there.

It's not easy, having Nobel genes that won't cooperate. Once when I was tired and my head hurt from too much calculus, I suggested she try again—if she had another Nobel baby, it might work this time.

It was a stupid suggestion. Mom couldn't have another baby. Mom and I do fine together—we take care of each other. When she can't take care of me, I can take care of both of us, but a baby needs more. So I shouldn't have said anything. Mom just stared at me for the longest time, and then she started to cry. I'm always making her cry, no matter how careful I am.

I have a book filled with pictures and bios of Nobel laureates. The book was published ten years ago and lists everyone from the beginning of the Nobel Prize until the year it was published, so my dad is definitely in there. It sounds like a lot of people, but it's not that many, actually. And I could rule a lot of them out if I did some research.

Not all the Nobel laureates are men, of course. There are women in my book too, not many, but a few, and Mom always points proudly to them, saying they show women could do anything, even back in the Dark Ages—and she flips to the beginning of the book—when few women had the opportunity to go to college. Sometimes she stares at the pictures of the women for a long, long time. I think Mom would have liked to go to college. I guess she couldn't—she had me instead.

The Nobel book gives information about the laureates' education and their careers, their accomplishments and triumphs. It's funny, but I'm more curious about the mistakes of successful people, about their losses and broken dreams. No book ever lists those.

I think about my Nobel dad every day, although I've never met him and probably never will. I fantasize about the way he looks and the way he talks, and I wonder if I look like him. When I eat chocolate pudding, my favorite dessert, and I'm watching TV while I eat, not thinking about my dad at all, I sometimes suddenly start wondering if my dad likes chocolate pudding too. It's like he's always there, inside my head, jumping out at every opportunity.

Children usually look like their parents, at least a bit. Genes do that. My mouth is almost exactly like my mom's mouth, and my hair is the same color. So it should be logical that I could find a familiar nose in my Nobel book, or the right shape of an ear or an eyebrow, and I do, but there are just too many of them. One of the men in there is my dad, but it could be almost any of them. I flip through the book often, and I know all the pictures now. I think I'd recognize all these men if I passed them on the street. But I still don't know which one is my father.

It seems pretty hopeless that I'll ever meet him. Mom says that's how it's supposed to be. He doesn't know who I am, and I don't know who he is. I don't know who decided it should be that way, and I'm not happy about it. My mom says it's impossible to find out who he is, but I'm not so sure. I have a secret plan.

I read about this boy who found his father who was a sperm donor. He sent a sample of cells scraped from the inside of his cheek to a DNA center for analysis. Then he put the data into genetic databases people use to build their family trees, and he found his father.

That was a long time ago, and I read that it's not quite as easy anymore, but I'm sure I can find a way. I just need to raise money first. DNA analysis and database access are expensive.

When I was little and my mom first told me about my Nobel dad and showed me the book with all these strange faces, I started crying, because I wanted a dad and I didn't know which one he was. I didn't quite understand it all then, about the Nobel sperm bank and the Nobel genes, but I knew I wanted a picture of Dad in my room.

My mom did something really nice for me then. It was years ago when she could still go outside the house, and she took me to a store and let me choose a picture frame. Then we went home, and we cut out a picture of the Nobel Foundation logo from a magazine, and put it in the frame. It's a blue N inside a circle. We put it on my dresser, and my mom ruffled my hair and said it was the best she could do.

It helps. Even now, although I'm not a little kid anymore, it helps. When I lie in bed at night in the darkness and I can't sleep and I start thinking about my dad, where he is and what he is doing, if he ever thinks about me, I look at that picture. When cars pass by, their headlights hit the glass, and it flashes. It's like my dad winking at me.

# 2

Mr. Rawls, at the end of the street, left a huge note on his door the other day, saying PAPERBOY! RING THE BELL! And I did, although I was a bit nervous, in case I'd forgotten to deliver his paper one day or something and he wanted to complain.

Mr. Rawls was wearing pajamas when he came to the door, rubbing his eyes like he'd just woken up, and I was sure he'd tell me off for ringing the bell so early. But he just asked if I'd be interested in taking this job: feed the goldfish, empty the mailbox, and mow the grass while he was away for work a couple of weeks at a time, and he looked at me like grownups do when they're trying to decide if you're a responsible kid or a troublemaker.

I hesitated a second, because I needed to think and thinking takes time, at least when you're not a prodigy, and he said I could talk it over with my mother and let him know. He wrote down his phone number and said to have my mother call him if I wanted the job. He said he thought I was responsible because I've never missed a day with my paper route.

I could see he knew about Mom. Everybody knows about Mom, even though nobody except Drum, who lives above our garage, has seen her in forever. Mr. Rawls didn't ask, though, like a lot of people do, "How's your mom?" in that tone I hate, making me have to reply, all smiling, "Fine, thanks," because that's what they want to hear and it's the only thing I can tell them.

Maybe he offered me the job because he feels sorry for me; some people feel sorry for me because of Mom, but I don't care. This will help me get money for my DNA project and find my dad. It's going to cost a lot of money. It's the only way, though. I've tried using the computer to research the Nobel Prize winners and narrow down the list, but I haven't made enough progress. It's hard to know who to eliminate. They freeze donated sperm, so even those who died before I was born could have donated sperm long before then.

Mom didn't say anything when I told her about Mr. Rawls and the job. She just nodded, looking into the distance, and then she started questioning me on cosmology.

I knew most of the answers, but that's because I've finished the latest cosmology book I got us at the library, and she's just read the first two chapters, so it was all she could quiz me on.

The first two chapters are the most interesting ones anyway. It talks about the theory of the "primordial soup," how we all originally came from a mud pit— how three billion years ago chemicals and energy combined and somehow life on earth began, quite accidentally.

Three billion years is such a long time it almost seems like the dinosaurs were here yesterday.

Anyway, I told Mr. Rawls that I wanted to take the job and that it was fine with my mom, and he said that was great, but I should have my mom call him so he could be sure I had her agreement and there was no misunderstanding.

When I got home, I asked Mom to call him, and she nodded that she would, but she didn't. I waited until after dinner, and she still hadn't. If she doesn't do things right away, she never does them. So, while she was watching television, I brought the phone over to her and let it sit on the arm of the sofa to remind her. She looked at it and nodded, and kept watching television, and when I came back she was watching a documentary on pelicans, and she was crying and still hadn't touched the phone.

I wanted the job. I needed that job. So even though Mom was crying, I picked up the phone and called the number on the note.

Mr. Rawls answered, and I told him again that I wanted to take the job and it was fine with my mom, and then put the phone into her hand. I do that sometimes when I need Mom to call the school or something important. It's not easy, and sometimes she gets angry as well as sad. But I have to do it, because if she doesn't call when she's supposed to, the social workers might visit and threaten to take me away, or we might start getting formal-looking letters that scare her even more. We have to pay the bills, and we have to talk to the school, we have to do whatever it takes to make everything seem okay.

And sometimes that means Mom has to do the things she doesn't like to do.

It's hard to understand, all the things she doesn't do anymore because she doesn't like them. There are many things I don't like to do either, but I still do them.

Mom spoke to Mr. Rawls quietly, like her voice wasn't quite there. I could hardly hear her, so I wondered if Mr. Rawls could. But she said all the right things, and when she hung up I hugged her and said thank you, and told her maybe we could get a new magazine subscription with the extra money. She didn't cry, and didn't scream, but she looked sad. Not a lot sad, just a little. She touched my hair and told me I was a good kid, then pushed me away. I wasn't sure what that meant, if she was okay or not, so I watched her extra carefully for the next few days.

It wasn't always like this. When I was little, Mom would go outside. She'd go to the grocery store, we'd go to the library together, the bookstore and the park, even to the movies—lots of places. She even drove a car. It wasn't a very cool car, but she drove it, and we sometimes went on long drives going nowhere—just driving around.

"Nobel son!" she'd say, smiling at me where I lay on the floor playing with my Tinkertoys or drawing pictures. "Want to get lost?"

And we'd go for a drive just for fun, go places we'd never been before. Most of the time we drove out of town. We had no map and no idea where we were going. Sometimes we'd end up on an abandoned road somewhere—no cars, no houses. It was as if we were the only people in the world. Then Mom would look at me in the rearview mirror with a special smile and stop the car. She'd look around with a finger against her lips, hushing me, and I'd almost shriek with excitement as I undid my seat belt.

"Scoot over, kid," she'd say, winking at me, and I'd scramble over into the driver's seat to sit in her lap, my hands reverently clenching around the steering wheel.

"Ready?" Mom would ask, and I'd take a deep breath and nod. At first we'd just crawl along, and I'd try to be patient because I knew Mom was grinning, waiting for me to complain before she'd push properly down on the gas pedal.

"Mom!" I'd whine when I couldn't stand it anymore. "I can *run* faster than this!"

Mom would laugh, her arms squeezing my middle in a hug and her nose burrowing through my hair as she kissed the top of my head. "Sure. But can you drive faster than this?"

"Mom!"

And we'd go a little faster, and then faster than that. I'd turn the radio up loud and open the windows, because it felt more real that way. I'd zigzag along the road if there weren't enough turns for me, make random turn signals, play with the window wipers and honk the horn, scaring the birds out of the fields and making Mom laugh even harder.

We had so much fun getting lost.

I wish we still did that. I'm big enough now to reach the gas pedal, so I could drive myself, and Mom could be in the passenger seat. But we don't even have the car anymore. When I got bigger and could do stuff for her, Mom didn't have to go out so often. It happened so slowly that I didn't realize it until it was too late and we no longer went for drives just to get lost. Then Drum moved into the garage and could do the adult things I wasn't allowed to do, so Mom no longer had to go anywhere anymore, and Drum sold the car for us. Now she won't go outside at all, even when we really need to do something, like buy me new clothes when I grow out of the old ones. That was a problem at first, but it's okay now. I learned how to buy clothes on my own, and Mom orders hers from catalogues.

When Mom sold the car, she got me a game console with the money. I'd wanted one for ages, but Mom didn't think it was educational enough. So I was sneaky and found an article in a magazine, about how computer games can enhance hand-eye coordination and improve problem-solving skills.

Mom chuckled and ruffled my hair when she finished reading the article, so I thought she was onto me. But the next time Drum did errands for her, one of the things he brought home was a brand-new console and a couple of games. The racing game and the flight simulator were my favorites. Mom used to play them with me, especially the racing game. We'd sit on the floor with our backs against the sofa, giggling and shouting, and race until Mom's egg timer beeped, because I was only allowed to play for an hour at a time. Mom got really good at racing. She could even beat me sometimes. But I don't play much anymore, and the console is dusty under the television. The games I have are mostly for little kids.

We don't have a lot of money, but we're not quite poor either. We have our house and we can pay the bills, and we have enough to eat and money for clothes and books and stuff. Mom doesn't work, but we still get money from somewhere every month. It's enough for us to live on, even with all of Mom's cigarettes and liquor and all the books and magazines, but there never is anything left for big things, like a new television or a better computer.

I don't know where the money comes from, and I only tried asking once. Mom didn't like the question at all. When I first found out about the money, I used to think it had to come from my Nobel dad, but now I don't know. I know so little because I can't ask Mom about things like that. I can only ask her about things like science and nature and history and literature. Asking her the wrong question is like pushing her down stairs, or punching her in the face, and it's so hard to know which question is the wrong question, so I try not to ask any questions at all.

We read about eugenics in school today. I think I may be a eugenics baby. Mom chose the Nobel sperm bank because she wanted a better baby, a genius baby. That's what I'm supposed to be: Mom chose my genes so I'd be a better person. The book said eugenics was bad, that it wasn't fair to put such a tag on people—that some people were better than others. I'd think that also means it isn't fair to say some genes are better than others.

I told Mom we were studying eugenics, and she looked up from *New Scientist* and seemed interested. "That's what Hitler wanted to do," she said. "He wanted to eliminate those he thought were inferior, and create a master race of what he thought were superior people." She shook her head. She seems to agree that eugenics is bad.

I wanted to ask Mom if making me wasn't eugenics, but I guess she didn't want to eliminate anyone; she just wanted to create one superior person, and maybe that's different. I hope so.

I'm feeling bad about forcing Mom to talk to Mr. Rawls. I'm mean to Mom sometimes. It's a burning feeling that sometimes feels good in a nasty way, and sometimes just horrible. It's little things, like "forgetting" to buy things she needs, or staying out when I know she needs me to do something, like go to the post office or the store.

I guess I'm hoping she'll decide to go out herself rather than wait for me, but that's stupid. She never leaves except when I go with her to her doctor's appointments, so she can get new prescriptions for her pills. And she doesn't do that very often either; most of the time she just phones in. The doctor's appointments are the only times she's left the house in two years.

Except for those two times on the stretcher.

When I do that, stay away from the house on purpose even though I know she needs me, eventually I start thinking about her on the stretcher, and I feel guilty about being mean to her, and start imagining what might have happened while I was away and she was at home, waiting and waiting for me. Then I run home as fast as I can, and the key doesn't fit the lock because my hands shake so much, and I push at the door and almost fall inside, and she's right there, standing by the door, waiting. Sometimes she's angry. Sometimes she's crying. Sometimes she stares at me like she doesn't even know who I am.

I prefer it when she's angry—angry is better than sad. I feel worse if she doesn't yell at me, and then I feel angry at feeling guilty and it all churns into a mess and I just go into my room and shut the door and crawl into bed with my Nobel book and look at my father's picture.

That's how I think about it: When I've looked through all the pages, all the pictures, I must have looked at my dad. I often look at my Nobel book at night, waiting for Mom to fall asleep. I have to wait, because I have things to do after she's closed the door to the bedroom.

Mom is never okay, and even when the lights are turned off and the house is quiet, she's not okay, and I have to go into the bathroom and count the pills, drift around the darkened house like a ghost to check her stashes of drink and prescription drugs, to make sure everything is where it's supposed to be.

I count the pills and write the numbers down, and I make tiny pencil markings on her booze bottles so I can see how fast they empty. Sometimes I replace a bit of the alcohol with water, so it's diluted and not as dangerous mixed with the pills, but I'm afraid to. She might find out, and I don't know what would happen if she realized I was interfering. It's safer just to watch and keep count, because if she doesn't know I'm watching over her, she won't be trying as hard to hide things from me.

Twice I've called an ambulance when a lot of pills vanished, twice I've stood over her in the middle of the quiet night and known that she would die then if I didn't make that phone call—it was my choice. Twice I've hated myself just for realizing I had a choice, but both times I made the correct one, the one worthy of a kid with Nobel genes.

# 3

Drum came to live above the garage two years ago. We put an ad in the local paper for a tenant, and he was the first one to call. Then he came over to look at the place, and he looked different from everybody else around here, with his leather jacket and long hair and black tattoos crawling out of his sleeves. He came inside and sat on our sofa, and it was very weird to see him there. It's strange to see someone in our house, because we're so used to being alone.

Drum didn't smile at all and didn't talk a lot, which my mom liked best of all. She wanted someone who wouldn't come knocking on our door wanting to talk, someone who wouldn't gossip at the grocery store. So she said he could have the place if he wanted it, and sent me out to show it to him.

He just glanced around up there once and nodded,

and went out to his Cadillac to get a few plastic bags from the trunk. And that was that. Now his car is in the garage instead of ours, because Mom stopped driving soon after. It's an old Cadillac, which is so cool even with all the rust and dents. Drum says it's "vintage" and doesn't even like to drive it to work, because he works nights and he says some drunk outside the pub where he plays might damage it. The car doesn't often leave the garage.

We don't see Drum a lot. He's just the guy who lives out there, whose drumming messes with my dreams and tricks my heart into beating faster. He calls himself Drum after his drums, but I don't think that's his real name.

Mom sometimes hates his noise and wishes he weren't there, but he's important, because he goes to the bank for her and pays the bills and other things that I can't do yet because I'm a kid. He also buys her booze, which I can't do yet either.

I'm glad I can't buy the booze. I can buy her cigarettes. They aren't supposed to sell them to me at the store, but this one lady does when no one else is around to see. She knows they're for Mom.

Once they showed this disgusting documentary at

school, and I got scared Mom would get cancer and die. I told her I wouldn't buy her cigarettes anymore; I told her that smoking was dangerous and she could get sick and die and that was why I wasn't going to buy them for her anymore.

She got really angry. Her face turned red and her hands clenched into white fists and she screamed at me. She got so angry she nearly hit me. She might have hit me for real if I hadn't run to my room and slammed the door shut and locked it. That was pretty bad, because she never hits me. She raises her hand sometimes, as if she's about to hit me, yells at me occasionally, but she never actually hits me.

She screamed and kicked the door for a while. Then she started crying, and she locked herself in the bathroom for so long that I got scared. The next day she was sorry and I was sorry. We didn't talk about it at all, but for Saturday lunch, she made me a big ice-cream sundae with bananas and kiwi bits in it, with lots of chocolate sprinkles on top. It was my favorite dessert when I was little, and Mom loved to make it for me. So in return I went out and bought cigarettes without her asking again. Getting them for her is probably less dangerous than not buying them. But I prefer it if Drum does it. He doesn't mind.

Drum also helps with the money. He pays rent, at least most of the time he does, when he has money and doesn't forget. I like having him there, even though he doesn't like kids and ignores me. He can be scary sometimes, but also kind of cool.

When some bullies from school followed me home one day last year, and I had a bloody nose because they'd said things about Mom and it was four against one, he was inside the garage with the door open, half inside the hood of his Cadillac.

They knew I didn't have a dad or anything and that my mom wouldn't come outside to help me or yell at them to go away, so they followed me all the way inside the yard, and didn't notice Drum was there.

They pushed me, so I fell. Then they cornered me against the front door, and one of them took my house key. That's when Drum came out of the garage, grabbed one of them by the back of his jacket, and blocked the others from running away. Drum looked really dangerous, and he grabbed the kid's hand and squeezed until he dropped the key and started screaming and cursing.

They all tried to get away, but Drum just stood there and they couldn't get past him, even four against one. Then he bent down and whispered something into the first kid's ear. Then he whispered something to the other three, one at a time, but I couldn't hear what he said.

The guys just stood there, staring at him and looking terrified, until he smiled this weird smile and stepped aside, hooking a thumb in the direction of the street. Then they took off, fast. They didn't even stop to yell back, like I thought they would.

Then Drum picked up the key and tossed it to me. He sort of looked at me—he never quite looks directly at me—and asked, "You okay, kid?" and I saw my front was covered in blood. It's amazing how much blood can come from one nose. I nodded, and Drum tossed me a roll of paper towels from the garage and told me to clean up before going inside.

Then he vanished into the engine of his car again, and it's the only time I've ever talked to him more than just saying hi or passing him messages from Mom.

I was afraid they would come after me the next day in school, for being a sissy and letting a grownup fight for me. But they didn't. They never came after me again, and neither did any of the others. They just looked at me in a weird way and avoided me, but they didn't even tease me about my mom for a long time.

Mom sometimes asks about my friends, and I tell her I hang out with them at school. I make it sound normal and she buys it, or maybe she just doesn't think about it a lot. She has enough to think about in the maze inside her head; there's not much room for other stuff. I don't have friends, not because I can't, but because I don't want to. I'd have to bring them home, that's what friends do, and they'd see Mom and they'd be embarrassed at the way she acts sometimes. I'm used to her, but they're not, and it would just be one big mess. They'd start whispering even more about me at school. I'm fine on my own anyway.

I wish I knew what Drum said to those guys. Sometimes I think it must have been magic. Some people think Drum is Mom's husband or her boyfriend, and sometimes I've imagined Drum could be my dad, even though he doesn't like me and doesn't act much like a dad anyway. But I'm pretty sure Drum has never won the Nobel Prize, and his picture is definitely not in my book.

I don't mind the drumming. It's not that loud, at least the neighbors hardly ever complain, and sometimes the rhythm helps me think, helps me keep one set of facts in my head while working on another and trying to make it all come together.

Sometimes, when things are bad and I'm scared, the drumming actually helps. It distracts me from the sound of my own heart, and when I don't hear my heart pound like a crazed animal is trapped inside my chest and trying to get out, somehow things seem a little bit better.

The best thing about Drum is that because he was here they didn't take me away when Mom went away on the stretcher those two times. I went with her in the ambulance to the hospital, and a social worker came to talk to me while I was sitting in the waiting room, pretending to read old comic books, waiting for them to pump her stomach and tell me she was okay.

The social worker was pretty nice, but I still didn't trust her. She took me to another room and we sat down in easy chairs and she asked me a lot of questions about me and Mom and how things were at home. My heart pounded while I told her lies, but at least I could tell her a friend of the family lives with us, so I'd be fine at home until Mom had recovered from her "accident." It was almost true, and she believed me.

The second time it happened, two people from Social Services came over and talked to Drum. He told them he didn't want to talk about Mom, her life was her business and he wasn't about to interfere. "I just live here," he said.

Then the social workers looked at me and frowned, and one of them wrote something down on her clipboard. I looked at Drum and was really scared, and he must have understood even though he didn't even look back at me, because he said, "I look after the kid when she's away, okay?" in a gruff tone.

They came inside and looked at the house, still writing things down. The house looked pretty good then, so I don't think they wrote anything bad down. They asked about my grades and if I liked school, and I showed them my last report card, and they smiled when they saw it and told me I was a bright kid. They didn't take me away after all. I guess things can't be too bad if you're doing well in school, so I'm glad I have my Nobel genes even if they're only good enough to give me A's in regular classes.

When Mom came home from the hospital last time, she had different medicine again. They often change it, but usually I don't see much difference. But this new medicine did something strange to her. Maybe it cured her for a while. I don't know if this is how she's supposed to be when she's okay. I hope not. But the amazing thing is that she went outside, alone. While I was at school, she knocked on the garage door and got Drum to drive her downtown.

Drum had a strange look on his face when they came back, sort of annoyance and worry, both at once, like he didn't like what was happening, but didn't know what to do about it. I'd just gotten back from school and was outside, just wandering around in shock because Mom wasn't there. I'd checked the yard and the garage and the street, and tried to think, wondering what to do, if I should go to the police or the hospital to check for her.

Mom jumped out of the car and hugged me, laughing and laughing, and I couldn't help but start to laugh too, even though I didn't even know why we were laughing. Then she pointed at Drum, who was opening the trunk of the Cadillac, and he made five trips to our door with buckets of paint while I just stared. Then I ran to help him, and the trunk of the Cadillac was filled with paint cans.

"This will be wonderful!" Mom said, laughing as she pulled all the paint into the living room, making a neat pyramid in front of our bookshelves. She yanked the drapes wide open, letting in sunlight for the first time in forever. A tornado of dust twirled around the room, but Mom was smiling. "No more darkness!" she shouted. "You're my Nobel son, you should have bright colors in your world, bright colors everywhere!"

Drum didn't come inside. He shut the door when he'd put the last pail of paint inside, and went back to the garage without saying good-bye, and I was glad he left, because Mom was acting so strange even though she was happy. The paint was all bright colors—yellow and orange and pink and green and blue. When I counted the stash, there were more than twenty cans of paint in Mom's pyramid. There was plastic, too, for covering the floor and the furniture, and rollers and paintbrushes and masking tape. Mom had thought of almost everything for once. It wasn't like Mom to think of everything. Maybe Drum had helped.

Mom laughed as she threw the plastic across the floor. "We're going to change our life!" she yelled as she poured the pink paint into a pan before we'd even moved the furniture out of the way. "Colors! Colors of living warm joy, colors of life and happiness . . ." She smiled at me, turning in circles and laughing up at the ceiling. "Pick your color, Nobel son! Any color you want!"

Our books and all the magazines made a plastic-covered mountain in the middle of the floor, and we just moved the bookshelves and the furniture around as we went along. We weren't all that organized. It all got messy, and paint got everywhere despite the plastic.

We painted far into the night, painted and laughed and drank soda and ate cereal out of the box, and Mom talked and talked and talked, so fast I could barely make out the words, but it didn't matter because she was laughing and I was laughing and there was bright paint everywhere. We even had a paint fight.

At around three in the morning I finally fell asleep, and when the alarm buzzed and I had to wake up to go to school, Mom was still painting, and she hadn't woken me up.

She likes to wake me up in the morning. She'll call from the door, in a soft gentle tone, call me baby, and tell me it's time to wake up. It's how she's always woken me up. It's silly now, but I don't mind.

But I can't count on her to wake me up. It's pretty random; sometimes she does and sometimes she doesn't. So I always set my alarm, too.

I still have the clothes I was wearing that night. I like to wear them sometimes on weekends, because they still have blobs of paint on them and remind me of how much fun we had. The paint has faded in the wash, but you can still see all the different colors. Mom sometimes smiles when she sees me wear them, even though she doesn't seem to remember that night anymore.

It turned out Mom's new pills weren't wonderful after all. She wouldn't stop painting. Days went by, and every time I came home from school, she'd chosen a new color. When she'd done the entire house, she started painting over the new paint with a different color. Sometimes she would start on the same wall again in a different color before it was even dry.

The house looked a mess, and Mom only went outside that one time, to get the paint. She didn't leave the house again for normal stuff, like going to the store. I'd hoped at first that everything would be okay now, that she could go outside and talk on the phone and do normal things, but she didn't. She still sent me or Drum out for everything, and all she did was stay inside and paint.

Bit by bit she got less happy about the painting, although she still didn't stop. She looked tired and didn't laugh anymore. Sometimes she seemed in pain as she dragged the paintbrush up and down the wall. It got scary.

After that she started to leave the house again, but it was in the middle of the night. Never in the daytime, never to do anything, just in the middle of the night, just to wander around the neighborhood. I was angry with myself for wishing she'd start to leave the house again; I didn't mean for it to be this way. But I knew it wasn't my fault—things don't happen just because you wish them. Not good things, and not bad things either.

Once the police brought her home. I hadn't been watching her. I was sleeping and didn't know she'd gone out. Then the doorbell rang and woke me up, and when I went to the door and peeked through the peephole, Mom was standing there between the two policemen, looking tiny even though she's still taller than me. She was wearing her nightgown and she was barefoot, and the cops had pulled her over for driving strangely. She'd taken Drum's Cadillac.

She smiled when she saw me, laughed and shook her head as she hugged me. She'd sleepwalked, she explained, and the police officers looked at me with pity and asked if my dad was home. I told them about Drum, that he wasn't home because he worked nights. I was careful to make it sound like he was Mom's boyfriend, sort of living with us, and they bought it. But if it happens again, next time they'll want to talk to him, and then we'll be in trouble.

Drum was furious when he found out she'd taken the Cadillac, even though she hadn't crashed or anything. He didn't scream or yell, but his lips were pinched so tight it looked like he didn't have any. He came to the door, and when Mom refused to come talk to him, he just yelled so she'd hear inside the house, and he shouted that if this happened again he would move away.

He also muttered that she was crazy, but only I heard that because I was standing by the door. I didn't like to hear it, and Drum noticed, because he glanced at me and said, "Sorry, kid," before yelling at Mom again, asking if she understood that if she touched his car again he'd leave.

She didn't answer, but when Drum had gone she started to cry, and I knew it was because she didn't plan to take his car, she didn't mean it, it just happened, and she couldn't promise not to do it again because it might happen even though she didn't want it to. And if Drum leaves she won't have anyone to do stuff for her that I can't do.

After that, Drum bought a padlock for the garage door and I got a security chain for our front door. I put it in place when Mom was asleep. I hope the sound of it wakes me up if she tries to go outside again in the middle of the night. I hope that works, because it's dangerous to go out like that, and besides, if she takes the Cadillac again and Drum leaves, we're in trouble.

After a while she stopped painting and went back to what she usually does, just sitting and watching TV or reading books or magazines. I guess the pills stopped working the way they did at first. The house still looked a mess, but I got used to it. It wasn't so bad—just different.

Most of the paint cans are still on our living room floor, but I've edged them behind the furniture or the closed drapes where they can't be seen, and thrown away the empty ones. I've taken the paintbrushes and the plastic and the other stuff and hidden everything away behind the washing machine.

I can't hide the half-painted walls, but I can't finish them either. I tried once, but Mom got too upset. I sometimes wonder if I should throw out the leftover paint, but I can't—it doesn't feel like we've finished yet.

# 4

Mr. Rawls left on his business trip today, and I went over there this morning to get the key. He showed me around. It's not a big house, about the same size as ours, but it looks empty, like he just moved in, although he's lived on this street for a long time. Maybe it's because he doesn't have any kids or a wife to mess things up.

He wants me to mow the grass once a week, and bring the mail in and feed his fish every day. I'm also supposed to check the temperature of the water to make sure the heater is working so the fish will be okay. "I don't want to come home to find them fried or frozen," he said, and made a face.

His aquarium is huge, with dozens of small fish in amazing colors. Some of them even have babies. It's beautiful, almost magical, like something from the television or *National Geographic*, and I could watch the fish swim around in there forever.

The fish tank is dirty, though. The glass walls aren't clear, and dead bits of plants float on the surface.

I guess Mr. Rawls saw me notice the dirt. He chuckled. "Not exactly sparkling clean, is it?" He shook his head. "I thought they'd make nice company without being high maintenance, but a tank of this size is a lot of work. I should probably get rid of it. Or get a small fishbowl instead, and keep just one or two. What do you think?"

I shook my head. "It's *so* cool! I think you should keep it."

"Cool, maybe. Filthy, absolutely. Ever cleaned one?"

"No." But I immediately started to wonder how it was done. Did you take the fish out first, and empty the aquarium of water? Or did you just scrub the glass with the fish still in there? What about the gravel at the bottom, how would you clean that? Or the floating plants?

Mr. Rawls looked at me, then at the aquarium. He reached out and tapped the glass, where it was turning green with algae. "If you think you can do it, that's another job for you. I hate doing it myself, and getting it professionally cleaned costs a small fortune. What do you say?"

I knew I'd like a job of cleaning the aquarium. I like figuring out how to do things, and I love to see things look like new after they've been fixed. It would be interesting to find out how to clean everything and still take care of the fish, so they wouldn't get hurt or die or anything.

"Sure," I said, hoping it would all work out and Mr. Rawls wouldn't come home to find his fish all dead in a squeaky-clean fish tank. "I'll do it."

"Great," Mr. Rawls said. He opened a cupboard under the fish tank and gestured inside. "All the cleaning things are there. I certainly bought enough of everything, and haven't used up much."

"Right now?" I asked. I wasn't ready.

Mr. Rawls shrugged. "Not necessarily. It'll keep for a while."

"I'll have to go to the library first and get some books, you know, read up on it. You know. To make sure I do everything right."

He looked at me funny as he nodded and said no problem. I guess not all people like looking everything up at the library, they just go online when they need to know something. Mom taught me to go to the library. Every time I asked a question she couldn't answer, she told me I could find out almost anything at the library, and I should come home with the answer the next day. We have a laptop computer, it's old and slow, but it works, and I can look things up on it. But the library's good too. I love computers; but it's fun to dig things up out of books.

Mom usually remembered to check up on me, to see if I'd looked up the answers to my questions. So I got used to always looking things up and reading about them when I wanted to know something, or if I needed to learn how to do something. That's how I know a lot of stuff other kids don't know.

I use the laptop a lot, for games and schoolwork and for finding out about things, and reading about Nobel Prize winners. Sometimes I write letters to my Nobel dad in my head, like the e-mails I would write if I managed to find him on the Internet, and imagine him sitting at a computer somewhere, or maybe on a train with his phone, reading my e-mail. Maybe he'd be sitting at a desk in a fancy office. Maybe he's a professor at a big university somewhere, with his own website listing all the discoveries he's made and all the books he's written and all the awards and honors he's won.

Maybe there would be a picture of his family on his desk, maybe a kid who looks a lot like me, and I'd suddenly have a brother or a sister as well as a dad. Even a stepmom, although I'm afraid to think about that, even just as a daydream inside my head, because I don't think Mom would like it at all if I had another mother, even just a distant stepmom on a website somewhere.

The letters I write to him in my head are often long—they'd be pages and pages and pages if I wrote them down for real—and sometimes I keep writing them in my head even after I fall asleep.

I often see my Nobel dad in my dreams.

"I wanted you to have the best genes money could buy," Mom is saying in my dream like she has so many times before, but now she's picking at my body, pulling tiny portions of me away and tossing them over her shoulder. "But they're not good enough. We have to replace them, you deserve better, you deserve much better."

My Nobel dad is standing behind her, frantically picking up the pieces and throwing them into an orange plastic tub that I recognize from my baby pictures. I was bathed in that tub; there are pictures of me naked and screaming, with soapsuds in my hair. Then the dream focuses on my Nobel dad as my eyes strain to know him, to memorize him. But he's a shadow, and whenever I focus on one part of him, it shimmers into nothing, and his face is only darkness.

Mom keeps picking at me, and my Nobel dad keeps picking up the pieces, and I feel myself falling apart, half of me missing, half of me gone, and I see everything in black and white, then everything fuses together in a gray blizzard, like white noise on television, and the last thing I see is the blinding flash as my Nobel dad smiles at me . . . but it's too late . . . I'm gone.

I'm sitting up in bed when I realize I'm awake, and the noise from the kitchen is familiar, the sound I also hear at school sometimes, when someone's brought a bag of M&M's and pours them on the table to sort into colors.

Mom is up again.

She went to bed hours ago, but now she's up again, and it's the middle of the night. That's a very bad sign. The familiar sound is an even worse sign.

I get out of bed and sit down on the floor by the door and rest my head against the wall. I always bring a pillow to sit on and a blanket, too, because when I have to sit here for hours, the floor starts feeling hard, and I get cold.

I open the door just an inch, and I keep the hinges oiled, so there is no sound. The gap gives me a partial view of Mom sitting by the kitchen table. I see her hands on the table and her legs under the table, and the many pill bottles and the small piles of pills.

She's going through the ritual. The full pill bottles are to her left, and when she's emptied them into another small mountain, she'll move them to the right. The table already looks like a caricature of the Rockies, but there are still several full bottles to go.

She collects pills. I don't think she's supposed to have that many of them, but she gets many prescriptions and she takes only some of them, and saves up the rest. She's done that for years and years. I try to throw away as much as I dare of the old stashes. But I can only throw away the pills she won't notice are gone, so maybe it's not much use.

Most of the time, all she'll do is play with the pills, like a little kid would play with a sticker collection or a coin collection. She'll sort them by color and size and shape, and by a special system that took me a long time to decipher. I eventually figured out she was sorting them out by how dangerous they were, how easy it would be to use them to get taken away on a stretcher again.

Sometimes she'll sort them to form pictures on the table, silly pictures, like a child's drawing of a house, or a face with a contorted smile.

Sometimes words. Sometimes the Nobel logo.

Sometimes she'll fall asleep right there at the table, and it'll be okay because it's just an alcoholic sleep, not drug-induced. I put the pills back so she doesn't even remember anything about them in the morning.

Sometimes she'll sort the pills back into their original piles and brush them off the edge of the table into her palm, then tip them back into their boxes and bottles and put them away, sighing as she closes the bathroom cabinet. I've seen her rest her palm on the closed cabinet door, like she's saying a reluctant good-bye.

I always check afterward if she put everything in the correct bottle so she won't make any mistakes later and take the wrong pills at the wrong time, or the wrong amount or something. I have a book I stole from the library, so I could make sure. The bottles are labeled, of course, but when Mom hasn't put them back right, it can be tricky to figure out which of the pills belong in which box. The book has pictures, so that helps, although many sorts of pills look almost the same.

The pill book is the only thing I've ever stolen, but I didn't dare check it out, because the librarians looked at me funny before, when I checked out medical textbooks to try to figure out what was wrong with Mom, and if it was hereditary and all that. I told them I was doing a paper on mental illness and they seemed to buy that, but I don't want people to talk about me at the library, too. It's bad enough at school and in the neighborhood.

I didn't like to steal. It's not the kind of thing a Nobel son would do, but the pill book was necessary. It has pictures of what pills look like and how to recognize them, how they work and how they can be dangerous, and I needed to know. Most of Mom's pills are in that book. A few aren't, or they look different, maybe because the book is a few years old, but I can still figure it out. I hope they don't change the pills so much that I have to steal another book.

Usually Mom's play with the pills is just play. But sometimes, twice now, she has started putting the pills in her mouth, a handful, and she chews on them and swallows, then another handful, and I feel the pills get stuck in my own throat while I wait and watch and my heart seems to be beating in my ears instead of my chest, and when she staggers back to bed or to the bathroom or falls asleep at the table without throwing up or spitting them all out again, it's time for me to run out and grab the phone, make that call for an ambulance.

This is the third time.

# 5

After Mom has been taken away on the stretcher, Drum and I sit in the living room, and there's silence for a long time. He's staring at the carpet, and I wonder what he's thinking—I'm afraid it's bad.

He doesn't want to get involved, but now he is—he's sort of pretending he's mom's boyfriend and that he'll take care of me, so I won't be left alone in the house.

There's silence, and I just sit there and wait for him to say something, because I don't want to risk being the first one to say anything. I'm worried about my mom, but the worry isn't that big now that the ambulance has taken her away to the hospital, because this is the third time and she was okay both times before.

Finally Drum stops staring down at the carpet and

looks up. He starts looking around—he hasn't been in here for a long time—and he stares at the half-painted walls. Now I see them with a stranger's eyes.

I'd gotten used to it, but it looks pretty bad.

We didn't have a ladder, and the walls are only painted as far up as we could reach with our brushes and hand rollers. At the time I didn't care—Mom was laughing, she was happy. She was talking too fast for me to answer, but we had colors and sunlight and laughter and the world was a vibrant rainbow, glittering with wet paint.

Now the paint is streaky, uneven, and in places transparent. Different colors lie on top of each other; some walls are in two different colors, others are in seven colors. There are places where the colors have run together into muddy dark shadows.

Drum shakes his head. "Don't take this the wrong way, kid," he says to me, and he's almost smiling as he gestures around at all the different colors on the walls, "but your mom is pretty nuts."

"I know," I say, and suddenly the half-painted walls are funny, and I smile and Drum grins. But then I feel bad inside for having smiled because I remember the way Mom's face sparkled with laughter when the world was a smudged rainbow, and I also remember the way her face looked gray like a rain cloud when they wheeled her out of here tonight.

"I guess you're not sleepy?" Drum asks.

I shake my head. I'm tired, but I feel like I'll never be sleepy again. It's like the need to rest is in my muscles, but not in my brain.

Drum stands up and keeps looking around, and he notices the pile of paint cans I stacked behind the sofa. He pushes the sofa away from the wall and starts checking out the cans. He lifts one up to read the label, then opens it and sticks a finger in the paint.

"Still usable," he murmurs, wiping the green finger on the knee of his jeans. He yanks the lid off another can. The paint is bright pink, and Drum shakes his head in disgust. "What do you say we finish the job, kid?" he asks, opening a third can. "It's not like we can make it any worse than it already is. Where are your paintbrushes?"

I show him the remaining paint cans and the painting gear in plastic bags behind the washing machine. Drum frowns as he rummages through the bags, and when he tosses the paintbrushes and rollers in the steel sink I see why. Most of them are useless. I didn't clean them after Mom stopped painting, and they are stiff with dried paint.

"Can't we use them?" I ask tentatively.

Drum shakes his head. "Nah. Best just to throw most of this junk away. I've got things out in the garage we can use instead."

Drum gets white paint from the garage and mixes it together with Mom's bright colors, to create soft shades that fill the house with light and air, pushing out the bright, bold colors that all of a sudden remind me of a clown's costume.

He brings a stepladder, too, and an extension pole, so we can paint all the way up to the ceiling, and we're careful not to add any more blobs of paint to the furniture or the carpet. Drum even shows me how to clean the old paint off the furniture, but it doesn't always work. Some stains won't come off, no matter how hard I try.

"What about your room, kid?" Drum asks, and I hesitate. I'm nervous to show Drum my room, the picture of the Nobel logo, the science books and the chemistry models, all the nerdy stuff that isn't very cool at all.

Drum shrugs and turns to the kitchen instead.

"Over here," I call. I throw open the door to my room and decide I don't care if he thinks I'm a geek. I want a new color in there.

Drum walks into my room, and it seems to get smaller with him there. He looks around but doesn't make any comment. "Okay. Which color do you want?"

I can't choose. We try many colors; we mix colors together and paint little squares on the wall until it starts to look like the old quilt on Mom's bed, but I still can't make up my mind.

Drum laughs at last, a rusty sound that reminds me of his Cadillac, then he pushes me out of the room and tells me to go paint my mom's bedroom some nice color. I leave him to it, relieved, trusting him to know my colors better than I do.

Drum puts rock music on and we paint all through the night, just like Mom and I did once.

This time the rainbow is perfect.

Mom is in the bed farthest away from the door, by the window, and I walk inside the room and straight to her, careful not to meet anyone's eyes. There are many people in the room, visiting the woman in the other bed.

Mom always looks tiny in a hospital bed, even though this one is so narrow that I can't comfortably sit on the edge like she wants me to, but there's no chair left—the other visitors have taken them all.

I put her favorite chocolate on the bedside table and stand there for a minute, wondering if I should go out to the hallway and see if I can find another chair. Then one of the other visitors pushes a chair to me with a smile, like he's apologizing for stealing it. I nod and sit down.

Mom smiles without looking at me, concentrating on the candy I brought her. She tears the wrapping slowly off the chocolate, into long curling pieces of paper, until she's exposed about an inch. She breaks off a piece and offers it to me, but I shake my head.

Now that I'm safely sitting by the bed, and have made it here without any questions or whispers, I'm glad there are so many people here. The more people, the less talking, fewer lies, less touching and smothering hugs. If we were alone, she might start telling me she didn't mean to do this—never defining "this," never explaining how it happened *accidentally* again.

She'd stroke my cheek and tell me she loves me, she'd tell me I'm her little Nobel son and I'm all she has to live for. She only does that while in the hospital. When she's back home, things go back to normal, and we never mention the hospital or the "accident" again.

I brought magazines. I bought them at a newsstand on the way from school, and I get them out of my bag and fan them out in front of her on the bed. That's part of the ritual. This is the third time, so I guess it's a ritual by now.

I got three magazines. One for her, one for me, and one for whoever finishes first, so neither of us has to wait for the other to finish. Three magazines are enough reading material to last a long time.

Mom likes most science magazines, but she loves the nature magazines most. I brought *Scientific American* and *Nature* and *Newsweek*. Mom gets to pick first, and she grabs *Nature* like I expected her to, and I start on *Newsweek*, waiting to see if Mom has a problem with that.

Most of the time she likes it when I keep up with current affairs, reading newspapers and magazines and watching the news channels. Other times she rips the magazine or the paper out of my hands and tears it up, screaming that this world is too horrible for children, that I shouldn't read something like this, shouldn't watch the television news or touch the papers, I should be a *real* child, an *innocent* child, I should live in a wonderful, warm place of bright colors and sunny skies and no worries.

I don't think it's fair that she's angry with me for living in this world the way it is, because that's not my fault, not the way the world is, or that I'm living in it, but I guess not much in life is fair anyway.

This time she doesn't mind me reading about war and politics. She concentrates on her own magazine, but I don't think she's reading. Her gaze doesn't move, just focuses on a spot in the upper left corner of the page.

I try to concentrate on an article about East Africa, but my head hurts and my shoulders are stiff because I hardly slept at all last night and still went to school as usual.

This is the third accident, and now I'm afraid the social workers will take me away and then Mom will be all alone, and I will be in foster care or something. I wouldn't have my paper route or my job with Mr. Rawls, and I'd never be able to get enough money to find my Nobel dad.

I hope Drum will be enough. I gave them his name,

even called him "Mr. Drum," so I wouldn't have to admit I didn't even know his name, and I told them he always looked after me when Mom was out of the house.

I didn't tell them the only time she was ever away was when she came to the hospital.

When I get home today after school and after visiting Mom, Drum calls to me from the garage. I go over there, and he talks to me while he waxes his Cadillac, his long hair hanging over his eyes and his voice disappearing under the car in a strange echo when he bends down to polish the hubcaps.

"The social workers were here today," he says. "About you."

He stops waxing and throws the rag away and folds his arms on his chest and really looks at me, and then it gets scary because he looks like a real adult with serious things to say.

"I can't keep covering for you, kid. I'm sorry." He shakes his head, and for a moment he looks sorry; then he just looks annoyed again. He grabs another rag and rubs at the car. "I don't want this. I can't do this." He curses. "I don't want my name in their files, them running background checks on me. . . . I don't want this responsibility. Do you understand?"

I don't say anything.

"What I'm trying to say—next time I won't do it. I won't. It should be their job, not mine. Understand?"

I shake my head. There are words inside, but I don't know which ones, so I can't speak them and they're just stuck down there, rubbing against the inside of my throat with every breath.

"They aren't evil, you know. You've got nothing to worry about. It's their job to look after kids like you." My stomach hurts bad when he says that, especially as I can see that he doesn't understand at all, that he doesn't understand that they can't take me away, that Mom won't make it without me, that it can't possibly work that way.

I want to say all that, but I can't, and then Drum throws me a bottle of window cleaner and his voice is lighter again. "Hey, I'll pay you twenty bucks if you get all the car windows really clean. What do you say?"

Twenty bucks is far too much, and I'm angry and don't want to get money just because he isn't going to help me. But I don't argue, because I need the money. It's more important than ever now to find my dad.

So I just grab a rag and go to work without saying another word.

We work for an hour in total silence, and when the windows and the mirrors of his car are all sparkling, Drum makes a paper airplane out of a twenty-dollar bill and throws it my way.

I'm rude and storm away without saying thank you, but I guess he doesn't care.

Mom's been in the hospital for three days, and Mr. Rawls got back today, two days ahead of schedule. I saw his car in the driveway, so I just dropped off the paper and didn't take in the mail this time, but he noticed me out the window and waved me inside. He was impressed with the fish tank. I cleaned everything, all the stones and the gravel and the plastic toys. I rinsed the plants, and the glass was shiny. It wasn't that difficult. It just took awhile.

"And you didn't even kill one of them," he said, laughing. "I expected to come back and find at least one or two floating belly-up. How much do you charge for that?"

I didn't know what to say, so I shrugged. Mr. Rawls said that if I committed to cleaning the aquarium

monthly, he'd pay me half of what he'd pay profes-
sional cleaners, on top of what he pays me for mowing
the lawn and getting the mail. Then he handed me
the money, and it was much more than I'd expected.

If he pays me this much every time, it won't be
long until I can complete the first part of my plan and
get my genes analyzed. After that, I'll work on the
next part: earning enough money to get access to the
genetic databases. It's like what people do when they
climb Mount Everest: they head for one camp at a
time, and the summit is the final goal out of many.

Then Mr. Rawls, like everybody else, asked how my
mom was, if she'd be coming home soon. He'd heard
already. Everybody knew she was at the hospital. My
teachers, too, and the kids at school. It's not that bad,
though. Since Drum scared the bullies off, nobody's
been that nasty. The kids in my class whispered and
stared a bit the first few days, but it was okay—if I
tried hard I could imagine they weren't talking about
me at all. The teachers gave me strange looks and a
lot of shoulder pats, and they looked surprised when
I turn in my homework like usual. I don't know how
people always find out things like that. It's like little
birds really do tell.

Today Mom is home when I get back from school. When I open the door and smell the cigarette smoke, I'm happy and angry both at once. Or maybe I'm just not sure which it is. Sometimes my brain isn't quite sure what I'm feeling.

Mom hugs me as soon as she sees me, but not very tightly. She's just arrived, and there's someone else here with her, a nurse or a social worker or something, but it isn't too bad. She just asks a few questions and then leaves, patting Mom on the shoulder and saying she looks forward to seeing her downtown next week, so I guess Mom is scheduled for some appointments.

Mom doesn't mention the newly painted walls at all. Our living room looks different, not only because of the new paint, but also because all the paint cans are gone from behind the sofa and the drapes, so the sofa is back in its right place, and the curtains don't bulge, but she doesn't seem to notice any of that.

I do my homework before dinner, and a chemistry problem has me stumped. Maybe because I've got other things on my mind. Mom notices me sighing and groaning, and she stops smoking and even stubs out the cigarette. She likes to help me with my homework. When I was in the first grade we'd do my homework together, lying on the floor like two little kids. Then Mom decided I needed to learn to work independently, so after that she'd help me only if I asked her to, or if I seemed to be having trouble. Sometimes I ask even if I don't have trouble.

"What's the problem?" she asks, looking over my shoulder at the book.

"It's chemistry," I tell her. "I stink at chemistry."

"Of course you don't," she says, as if it's absurd. "You have Nobel genes."

That's exactly why chemistry makes me angry. Because I *should* understand.

I throw down my pencil. "I don't want to be a genius, Mom! I just want to be me."

Mom looks at me with her eyebrows raised. "That's not logic worthy of a child with Nobel genes." She pulls up a chair and grabs my book. "You can find yourself a more worthy goal than that. Now, let's see. . . ."

The chemistry problem gets solved with Mom's help. Sometimes the drugs cloud her brain so she can't even think properly, and then she can't help with homework. That always makes her cry, so I'm glad the new drugs don't do that.

After I finish my homework we don't talk anymore, and I make us sandwiches for dinner while she flips through some of my other schoolbooks. Later I'll ask her about some other homework stuff even though I'm not having problems with it, because helping me makes her feel good.

While we eat, I finally ask her if she likes the new colors. She looks around, surprised, and then nods and says it's nice. She doesn't ask how we did it or anything. I guess she doesn't care.

Mom has more medicine. Different medicine. I don't quite understand why they keep giving her more when the pills keep sending her to the hospital and she almost dies.

Maybe this medicine isn't as dangerous. That could be the reason. And I guess she has to have the medicine even if it can be dangerous. Just like people have to have cars and booze and cigarettes and chainsaws, even though it's all dangerous.

Still, my stomach hurts as I watch her put the new pill bottles in the bathroom cabinet. She doesn't throw away the old ones. She never does, and I can't get rid of much. I don't dare touch anything she sees every day.

I look the new drugs up in my stolen book after Mom has gone to bed. I look up the dosages, the side effects, and the interaction with other drugs and with alcohol, and I write it all in my old math book, even though I think I'll always remember everything about her pills.

# 6

I was worried the new pills might make Mom start painting again, like the last ones did, ruining the new walls Drum and I made, but they don't. They don't seem to make much difference at all. Mom isn't laughing, but she isn't crying, either.

From what I read about the new medication, it seems they've diagnosed her with something new again. Or maybe they're just experimenting because they don't know what to do. Most of her drugs are for depression, but this one isn't specifically for depression. It can help with many different problems, like phobias and compulsions. So maybe it's for her agoraphobia. Maybe it will help her leave the house again.

It's weird to think about it—that the way my mom acts and the things she does aren't really her personality, the way she really is deep down. It's fake, it's a disease, chemicals running wild in her brain and causing mayhem instead of doing whatever it is they're supposed to.

But what is left, then? If this is all a disease, not my real mom, then where is my real mom?

Maybe I won't meet my mom's real self until they find the right medication, but if it's medicine making the chemicals in her brain right, how can that be the real person?

It gives me a headache to think too much about this, but my brain still keeps going back to it. Maybe I think about it so much because many diseases are hereditary, and I want to be prepared if it starts happening to me.

It's sort of like my Nobel genes. Am I the real me, or is the real me the genius my Nobel genes were supposed to create?

The new drugs aren't working. At least, not that I can see. Mom doesn't do much of anything. She doesn't even much read the science magazines anymore, even though I buy her new ones every week. She sits in her easy chair, the TV is on although she doesn't watch it, and she's started to play a lot with my pin-cushion toy. You can push your hand or an object into the surface of the pins and on the other side, a three-dimensional picture forms. I used to think it was so cool when I was little.

Mom likes to push at the pins and create a picture, something she makes up in her mind, then look at the other side to see what came out. Sometimes she starts laughing and shows it to me. Usually I can't see the same thing she sees, but I always pretend I do.

Mom often told me the pins were like genes. They could form different kinds of pictures. She thought I could make any kind of picture I wanted. I had *potential*. She said I just had to make up my mind what I wanted to be, and then let my good genes take me there.

But it's not quite that easy after all.

Mom has also started playing Tetris a lot. It's a handheld game she got me for Christmas many years ago and I'd almost forgotten I had it, but she found it somewhere and hasn't let it out of her sight since. She can play for hours, for days, but she doesn't care about the score. Sometimes she'll just stop in midgame for no reason, even if she's close to breaking the high score.

I could never do that. I love breaking high scores.

Mom doesn't seem to actually like playing the game, like I love playing computer games. It's just something she does instead of staring into space and smoking.

I don't like Tetris, because there's no way you can win, no real end to the game, so you always, *always* lose in the end, no matter how well you do or how good you get.

But I like it that she plays, because she doesn't smoke while she plays. I don't like breathing in cigarette smoke, although I should be used to it by now. When the batteries run out on the Tetris game, the house fills up with smoke again. I have to make sure she always has plenty of new batteries.

Mr. Rawls should be back tomorrow evening. I keep counting my money, and I get the same results: I can soon buy the DNA analysis, the first part of my plan. The first step toward finding my dad.

I'm trying to keep my hopes down, though, because it may not work. But it's a strange thing about hope: It's a hard thing to kill, even when you know how bad disappointment can hurt.

I go to sleep thinking about my dad, making plans

of how I'll find him. I'm thinking too much when I fall asleep, and in the middle of the night I wake up from a nightmare, sweating and breathing the way Mom sometimes does, hyperventilating, and the room is spinning around me and I want to scream, but I know that won't help. I know that everything bad passes if I just wait, and I calm down.

It was the old dream, the one that always tells me the same thing, that it's *my* fault Mom is sick, that she's sick because I'm not the genius I was supposed to be, because I'm not a real Nobel son. I hate it when the dreams tell me this.

I know I won't be able to fall asleep again, so I turn on the light and reach for my Nobel book. I've been spending a lot of time with my Nobel book lately, working on eliminating as many men as possible and coming closer to finding my dad.

I get a funny feeling inside when I think that far ahead. What will I do when I have had the DNA analysis done and entered the information into the genetic databases and narrowed it down to four, or two, or one? Will I write to them for real, like I've done so often in my head, asking if they could be my father?

What if I find my father? Will he want me? Will he, like Mom, be disappointed that I'm not a genius?

When I think about it too much, I almost don't want to find my dad anymore. But that never lasts long. When I look at my Nobel picture and flip through my Nobel book, I know I want it more than anything.

It doesn't matter that he may not want me. I want to find him anyway.

I have to know where I came from.

I have to label my Nobel genes.

# 7

I'm a lie.

The Nobel sperm bank doesn't exist. It never did.

I stumbled on it yesterday. I'd read about the Nobel bank many times online before, mostly people talking about the ethics of it. Most people thought the bank really did exist. But yesterday a new article popped up in my search, a really good one and well researched, and there's no doubt: The Nobel sperm bank is a myth. Someone once tried to create a bank like that, but it didn't work out. The bank my mom told me about never existed at all; no sperm bank ever stocked the genes of hundreds of Nobel Prize winners. No Nobel kids were ever born.

None of it is true.

At first I couldn't believe it, couldn't believe Mom would lie to me about something so important. But then I got furious at myself, because all of a sudden it seemed incredibly stupid to have believed this all my life, to have never doubted anything she said. I should have realized; it was stupid of me to believe it for so long. I wasn't a "wonderful dream come true" like she told me so often with a smile and a kiss to my forehead.

I suppose I could be a regular donor baby, but believing that seems almost as stupid as believing the Nobel lie. It's all a lie. I wasn't her fondest wish. I was probably an *accident* that she wished had never happened, wished so badly that she made up a story to believe in.

And what about my dad now? Where is my dad? Did he even know about me? Did he want to know about me?

I can't stop thinking about it, about how I came to be. Movies play inside my head, all sorts of stuff that might have happened: my mother tells my father about me and sometimes he smiles, sometimes cries, sometimes yells, sometimes he even hits my mom and I get angry with him, which is pretty stupid because it's just my imagination. It's harder to picture him now, no longer a jumbled-up picture of all the black-and-white scientists in my Nobel book, just a gray shadow.

I don't know what to do now.

At first I was so mad at Mom for lying to me. I almost rushed to her room and started yelling, but I forced myself to sit down first and think it through, and after a while I realized it may not be like that at all. I'm not sure she even knows she's lying to me. I think Mom thinks the Nobel lie is the truth.

Either way, I know she'd cry if I told her. She'd cry and then maybe, if I was very lucky, she'd stop crying and get angry, and we'd never talk about it again. We'd pretend it never happened and that I still had my Nobel dad somewhere out there, only we'd both know it was a lie, and that would be even worse.

That's the best-case scenario. With my mom, pretending is easier than the truth. The truth can send her to the hospital on a stretcher with a mask over her face.

I want to change my room. I want to get rid of the Nobel picture and the Nobel book, all the Nobel lies, but if I don't want Mom to notice, I have to do it carefully. I've already shifted the picture frame with the Nobel logo so my Nobel dad won't wink at me at night. Mom would notice if I threw it away or put it out of sight.

Mom doesn't often come into my room, but she stands in the door at night when she thinks I'm sleeping. She checks up on me five times, unless she's too out of it on pills or alcohol. I know, because by now I always wake up. She'll stand in the door, silhouetted by the light behind her, and stare at me while I look back at her, my eyes half-closed as I pretend to sleep. Most of the time she just looks in for a second and then leaves. But sometimes she stays longer. She'll stand so still I'm often not sure if she's breathing, and sometimes I'm convinced it's a dream because no human being could stand that still for so long.

Then she'll sigh, just loud enough for me to hear it, and pull the door closed. And then the muscles I didn't know were tense relax, and I sit up, inch out of bed the way I know how, the way no sound is torn from the bedsprings, and tiptoe to the door to make sure she's okay.

Last night, when I first realized that the Nobel bank was a myth, I got one of my attacks. They're panic attacks. I know that from looking it up at the library.

The first time it happened, I thought I was sick,

maybe even dying, but now I know it's just my mind tricking me into thinking something really dangerous is happening. Because I can't do anything about it, my body sort of pretends it's doing something. My heart starts slamming and I can't control my breathing and I start to see spots and can't stand upright and have to lie down.

I know how to deal with it now, so it's not that bad. I just lie down and wait for it to pass and try not to think, because thinking makes it worse. But last night, when my Nobel dad was suddenly taken away, it was impossible not to think, and it was pretty bad.

I hate my attacks because they make me wonder if Mom's sickness is also inside me, but I try not to think about it too much. I guess that's what Mom does, she thinks so much she gets all tangled up in her thoughts until she's trapped somewhere inside her own mind.

I'm again thinking about running away, but I know I'll never do that. I'm worried about leaving Mom alone, with nobody to measure the booze and count the pills, no one to make her sandwiches to eat in bed on those days she doesn't get up, no one to call the ambulance when she needs one.

I don't know what to do now. I feel like a different person, or *not* a person, like half my genes have been yanked out of me, replaced by tens of thousands of minuscule question marks, revolving around in confusion.

I have a dad somewhere. A real dad, a normal dad, not a Nobel dad. Maybe I have brothers or sisters. A real family, people whose smiles aren't a riddle, people who don't need to be watched over at night. I wouldn't leave my mom, but if I had a dad, another family to visit sometimes, then maybe everything would be easier at home, too.

When I finally leave my room because I'm hungry, Mom looks different, although she's just sitting there in front of the television like she normally does. She looks like a stranger, because she lied to me about something so important. I think I'm still angry inside, but it's hard to tell because I'm so confused.

It's Saturday, and I don't have to go to school. I can stay at home all day and stare at my mother and wonder why she told me I had Nobel genes. Most of all I want to ask Mom about my real father, and I flip through the options in my head, but I don't find a safe way. Words are fire hazards—they're risky, a trap.

I look away from the television and see that familiar pile of brochures lying on the coffee table, advertisements for courses and workshops and advanced classes, and it becomes hard to swallow my cereal.

I don't want to go to those anymore. I only went because of my Nobel dad. I wanted to learn a lot so if I ever found him we could talk about science and he'd be proud because I could at least try to understand his work; so that he wouldn't be too disappointed his son wasn't a genius. But now there's no point in trying to understand chemistry and physics and all that.

Maybe now, since I no longer have a Nobel dad, just being me isn't such an unworthy goal.

I try to figure out a way to tell Mom that, to somehow tell her that being *me* is good enough, but when I open my mouth the words stop before they emerge.

Mom looks up because I made a sound, and I just shrug. I can't tell her, can't ask her.

My Nobel genes are all Mom talks about when she's okay. All she does when she's happy is go through my scrapbooks, read books on stimulating intelligence, study science books and science magazines so we can talk about science and nature and fuel my genius genes.

Does it matter who my dad is?

Mom has taught me genes are important. Half of what I am came from my dad. But he came from his parents, and they came from their parents, and so on back through the ages, all the way back to the primordial soup I read about in the cosmology book.

That's how I must think of it. I came from a puddle of mud back at the beginning of time. Everybody did.

# 8

I can't stop thinking about my dad.

The primordial soup isn't enough after all. I reread the chapter in the cosmology book, lost myself again in the story of the amino acids, the proteins, the story of the building blocks of life created accidentally by random chemicals and bolts of lightning—but it isn't enough. My question marks keep spinning faster and faster and I *have* to find out.

I wish there was someone else I could ask, someone other than Mom. Someone who knew my mom back before I was born.

I used to ask about my grandparents when I was little, but Mom didn't like the questions at all. So I stopped asking for a long time, even though I really wanted to know, really wanted a grandma and a grandpa like almost everybody has.

Then last semester, when we were doing a family tree at school, a genealogy chart, I asked again about my grandparents, nothing big, just their names so I could add them to the chart. My family tree looked pretty silly with just the two of us.

Mom didn't answer, but when I asked again, she told me they were dead and that names of dead people don't matter, and she stormed into her bedroom and slammed the door shut. I had to make up names on my chart and keep watch that night.

Asking questions is never a good idea.

The picture of the Nobel Foundation logo finally goes in a drawer because I can't stand having it there in its usual spot, can't stand the feeling that the blue *N* is staring at me, mocking me.

Maybe I knew what would happen, maybe I put the picture away because I knew that sooner or later Mom would notice, and early one Sunday morning when she should be still sleeping, she is standing in the doorway to my room, staring at the top of the dresser where the picture used to be.

"Where's your Nobel picture?" she asks, and it seems like a sign. I thought Mom would sleep for another hour, so I'm sitting at my desk with my laptop, and I was rereading one of the stories about the sperm bank that was sometimes called a Nobel sperm bank, an article about the kids who were born off that project, and how they weren't actual Nobel kids. Mom's gaze is locked to the place where my Nobel picture should be, and she doesn't even notice what's on my screen.

Not yet.

The question marks twirl faster and faster inside me, howling in impatience. Their edges are getting sharp and they never, ever leave me alone.

Mom knows. Mom can tell me.

I don't think. I don't talk. I just tilt the laptop her way and stop breathing.

Mom frowns at first, her mouth opens. Then her face turns pale. She puts one hand on the back of my chair and the other one on my desk and bends down, reads the article, silently, slowly, like it's something new, a foreign language she barely remembers. Her eyes are wide open and her mouth moves to form some of the words as she reads them.

My heart starts to pound painfully loud as I realize my mistake.

This is all wrong.

Mom wasn't lying to me. She believed the story about my Nobel dad. She thought she was telling me the truth, and now I've ripped away the fairy tale we've lived in all our lives. Color is vanishing from her face; she's turning whiter as she reads, reminding me of the way she looked on the stretcher.

This is wrong. But she's still reading.

My ears buzz and my throat tightens. I can feel every heartbeat pushing blood through my body, feel the smooth surface of the computer touch pad under my cold fingers, feel every second stretch out infinitely—but now there's nothing I can do but wait. It's too late. Too late to dive for the off button, too late to slam down the laptop screen, too late to shove the computer off the desk and let it crash to the floor and break into a useless heap of plastic and metal.

I breathe. One quick, desperate breath, and then hold it again, the fresh scent of Mom's shampoo trapped deep in my lungs.

Mom reads the text on my screen slowly. She's used to ripping through a whole magazine in a couple of hours, while it takes me days, but now she carefully inches past each word. When she reaches the bottom of the screen, her gaze stays on the last line, and she doesn't move.

I know what she wants without her saying anything. My fingers move on the touch pad, scrolling down to display the rest of the story. It can't get worse than this, and she's still there, still alive and breathing and reading, and I start hoping. Maybe I'm overreacting. Maybe it won't be as bad as I feared. Maybe it won't be bad at all. Maybe she'll just smile and shrug and tell me the truth about what happened and who my real father is.

Mom's eyes start moving again when the rest of the article is on the screen, and she reads it all, then stands there unmoving, her gaze still stuck on the last line. There's nothing more on the page, but she stares at the last word, as if she's waiting for me to scroll down again.

Maybe she's expecting more—maybe she's hoping for a smiley face to pop up and stick its tongue out at us, saying it was a joke. Maybe she wants me to say it's a pretend article I wrote for school or something.

I could still say that.

Couldn't I?

I bite my lip hard, my shoulders are so tense they hurt. I wait for her to say something, do something—

for anything to happen—but nothing does. Mom just stands there, and I just sit there, until the screensaver kicks in and dice start tumbling across the starry sky.

Then she hits me.

It's so unexpected that it doesn't even hurt. She raises her bare foot and kicks hard at my chair. It shoots away from the desk and my arm bangs against the wall, but I don't stand up, I just stare at her, and everything's surreal, like one of my crazy dreams. Mom has never hit me before, never slapped me, never hurt me, but now there is steel in her eyes, like she hates me, like she wants to hurt me. She wants to hurt me bad, and she's coming at me.

"Mom," I say desperately, my voice a dull knife bouncing off the awful silence in the room, and she stops. Her eyes flicker for a moment, then turn icy again. She lunges at me in silence, not even screaming, her hands raised to hit me, nails like claws, like a rabid predator from a magazine picture, and I hunch down and raise my arms to protect myself against the blows. Another slap, something scratches my cheek, and the pain transforms my fear into fury that grows until it explodes and I burst out of my chair and stand up straight to face her.

I'm almost as tall as she is now.

My heart slams against my ribs in something that resembles joy far too much, because I'm mad. Now I'm furious enough to fight back, and I know I'm going to do it. She started it, and I'm going to hit her back.

I wait, wait for her to hit me one more time, and this time I won't just sit and take it.

She doesn't. Her arms fall to her sides, and she backs off. Her breathing is jagged, the sound almost a moan. She looks away from me, down, and her gaze falls on my computer, the stupid dice still rolling across the universe, hiding that horrible article.

I see her hand lift, but before I can react, she has grabbed the computer by the screen and tossed it aside. The screen swivels back with a horrible crunching sound. I grab the laptop and put it on the floor, slide it way back under my bed, out of her reach. I can't let her destroy it. It could still be a tool to find my dad.

When I turn around, Mom's gone.

I run after her, and for a few horrible moments the house seems empty. Then I find her in the storage room, pulling out the buckets of leftover paint, every move frenzied. A frown is pulling her eyebrows together and making her mouth look old.

I shed the last of my fury instantly; it falls on the floor and disintegrates. I'm ashamed. I knew. I knew my Nobel dad was a hope, a dream, a fantasy—not a lie.

Why did I do this to her?

I kneel beside her as she starts opening the paint cans, wishing I could take back everything that happened today, and whisper, *I'm sorry, I'm sorry*, but it's too late and she doesn't hear me, doesn't answer, doesn't say a word, doesn't seem to know I'm there. I try to take her hand, but she reaches for another paint can, shrugging my hand off without noticing me at all.

The taste of salt fills my mouth. My hands are cold and empty, useless. My head feels heavy. A drop of blood from where her nails scratched my cheek falls from my face and on the floor, but vanishes under a pool of green. Paint splatters all over the floor as Mom tears the lids off the cans.

Eventually I go back to my room, leaving Mom alone with the paint. My computer is okay. The hinge is broken, but that's it. I just have to be careful when I open and close it.

I sleep that night, but not well, and Mom doesn't check on me at all. Monday morning I leave the computer behind in my room when I go to school, hidden under my bed just in case. Mom is in the living room with the paint, she was there all night, and I don't say good-bye. I'm hoping everything will be back to normal when I get back.

When I come home from school Mom is singing, and I pause with the door open, listening hard. The singing can mean different things. It can be wonderful and it can be dangerous. It can turn into screaming or into laughter. It can mean Mom will cook dinner tonight and ask me to play chess, or it can mean she's sitting on the coffee table throwing pills up in the air and trying to catch them in her mouth. It can mean she'll watch TV with me and laugh in all the right places, or it can mean she'll throw a sheet over the television set and start shouting that I shouldn't watch TV because it shows a world too cruel and horrible for innocents like me.

By now I feel I should be able to tell the difference from her voice, her tones, her choice of lyrics, and I keep trying, but it isn't working. Not yet.

I peek into the living room, nervous about what

I'll find, but it's not too bad. She's painting the wall behind the television; the wall Drum and I painted a soft pink. But she's not just painting the wall a different color: She's painting a door, a small door, maybe half the size of a normal one, and she's good at it. Very good. The door is green, with a small glass window and an ornate knob painted in tan. It almost looks like a real door.

Mom can paint really well. I never knew that. I'm good at art in school, but Mom never liked it when I drew or painted at home, so I stopped doing it. When I bring my art projects home at the end of the school year, she throws them away, unless I like something well enough to hide it somewhere in my room. Mom always says it's a waste of my time and my gifts to play with paints. She wants me to read instead, or watch documentaries, or even just sit and think. When you're a genius, art isn't important.

But now it is. Now it's very important.

I don't have Nobel genes, but the genes that help me draw and paint better than everyone else in the class—I must have gotten them from my mom.

Good genes. Gifted genes. From her, not from a Nobel dad. It's an amazing and wonderful discovery.

I feel warmer, and the question marks inside of me don't feel quite as empty and angry anymore.

Mom notices me and smiles widely, waving at me with the paintbrush. She has paint all over her clothes, and smudges on her face, just like that time we painted the walls all through the night. The smile should relax me, but it doesn't—she's too happy, she's in that mood that crashes without warning into despair or anger or play with the pills. I smile back as carefully as I can, not too wide, but still wide enough, and walk to her.

"That's a beautiful door, Mom." My voice is quiet; I can hear the apprehension in it myself, but Mom smiles and looks at the door with pride.

"This is just the beginning," she assures me, carefully outlining a mail slot toward the middle of the door. "The beginning. Brand-new world, brand-new possibilities, everything new . . ." She looks up and smiles at me, her gaze seeing something far away. "It will be wonderful."

I nod and stand there, watching as she finishes the mail slot and starts on the hinges. She laughs. "I should have done the hinges first, shouldn't I, to keep the door upright? Still, it's all hanging together—quite a miracle, isn't it?"

I nod, then sit down and watch her paint. She's piled all the wall paint around her, and she has dug up my old painting kits, too. It's a mess, but the door is beautiful and Mom is happy and when she smiles like this, I love her, even though I know something is very wrong.

Mom keeps painting, even when it's dark, and neither of us gets up to turn on the lights. Mom doesn't mind working with only the faint hall light for illumination. She hums as she works on the door. Finally she stands up and stretches, smiles, and starts putting the lids on the paints. "The door is perfect," she says proudly. "Isn't it?"

"Yes," I say, because it's true. "It's perfect. It looks just like a real door."

Mom looks at me with a strict face that reminds me of when I was little. She hasn't looked at me like that for a long time. "No opening the door, Nobel son," she says. "It's not ready and the paint isn't even dry. You can't open the door until it's ready. Promise?"

My heart almost stops in my chest when she calls me Nobel son again. She's forgotten what she saw on my screen, and I'm so relieved.

I promise not to open the fake door, and Mom

smiles, comes up to me and hugs me, kisses my fore-head. She goes into the bathroom, and I clench my eyes shut as I picture all the pills, trying to remem-ber how many is safe. I must remember, I must keep count and make sure she's safe.

Mom keeps painting doors on the walls for the next few days. She doesn't even stop to talk or play Tetris or smoke, and I just go to school and come home like normal, still guilty over my huge mistake, too guilty to stay long at the library, too guilty to be mean by coming home late or not doing everything exactly the way she'd like.

She isn't smiling anymore like that first day. She paints the doors in silence, and they are getting less and less pretty. Some are just vague rectangles on the walls and she paints them fast, each brushstroke angry, and she hisses at me if I get in the way.

I just have to wait and hope everything goes back to normal.

Sometimes I don't like the way she's ruining the hard work Drum and I did on the walls. I liked it that our house looked normal, but while she's not playing with the pills, it's worth it. She doesn't want to stop to eat, so I make her sandwiches and bring them to her, put a plate down next to her, and she'll eat it absently when she pauses to change colors.

I stay in my room a lot so I don't remind her of what happened, hoping she's forgetting it all and we can go back to the illusion, back to my Nobel dad. I even put the picture with the Nobel logo back in its usual place. I buy groceries she likes, hoping she'll be tempted to cook dinner because she's always happier when she cooks. But she doesn't even notice, and we eat my version, maybe a little burnt sometimes, or too salty, but still, a version of her meals, her recipes.

Before, she would usually smile and acknowledge that I've tried to follow her recipe, but she doesn't now. She just stares into her plate and eats with a rhythm, chewing exactly eleven times between bites, and sipping from her glass of water every three bites.

The rhythm eating is a bad sign; there are many bad signs, but I try not to think about it. At least she's still painting the doors—she's not lying in bed with the lights out, she's not sitting at the kitchen table sorting her pills into neat little piles, she's not on the stretcher.

Again the wish comes creeping, the wish of running

away, finding a place of my own, a space where there is no mother to look after, no mother to worry about, no mother to keep alive.

I shove it away with all the anger I can force up—I won't leave her, I can't.

# 9

I made another mistake.

I should have made sure she had plenty of paint.

One day when I return from school some of the empty paint cans are outside the door, thrown there with force, splashing the few drops of remaining paint on the ground. Mom must have opened the front door. That hasn't happened in a long time.

I smell alcohol as soon as I step into the house, a sort of lingering smell underneath the usual paint fumes, and I only notice it because I suspected.

Mom has run out of paint, and I have a terrible feeling I know what that means—she has had time to think. She has remembered the website I showed her; she has remembered that my Nobel dad doesn't exist.

I haven't had to worry about the pills for a long time, but now I rush to the bathroom, and I don't even need to count. The cabinets are open and nothing's there, and I run to the kitchen and see the piles of remaining pills on the table.

Her bedroom. She's lying in bed, still and pale. She's breathing, but it doesn't matter how fast my heart is beating or how much I want her to wake up, her eyes don't open. It doesn't matter how much I shake her and slap her face—I hate doing that—she won't wake up, even when I throw a glassful of cold water on her face.

I grab the phone from the bedside table and make the call, and this time I leave her and sit in my room while I wait. I know I should sit with my mom, I should hold her hand and talk to her, will her out of the drug-death, but I can't. This time the guilt is all mine, nobody else to blame, but I still hate her, because if she hadn't done this, it wouldn't be my fault.

I spin my globe while I listen for the ambulance. I try not to think about Mom, but instead about where in the world my dad is and if he ever thinks about my mom and me. When the ambulance arrives, I'm glad they don't use sirens, because fewer people will notice. I open the door and point to Mom's bedroom.

This time I stay behind when the ambulance takes

my mother. I tell the crew about Drum, that he'll be back from work soon, and they nod and leave me behind without questioning, because they're in a hurry to save my mother's life.

When Mom's gone, my feelings come rushing back. First the shame of being angry at Mom, then fear of being taken away. I don't know how much time I have before someone checks up on me, so I rush to the garage, and slam my fist hard against Drum's door when knocking doesn't work. Drum works at night, so he sleeps during the day.

Drum finally opens the door a crack, scowling at me. He's wearing jeans but no shirt, and I probably woke him up, but I don't care. I don't know how fast things happen. They could be coming any minute now to take me away, and he has to help. He can tell them I'm fine here with him, and he can phone the hospital and they'll tell him about Mom if he's an adult and responsible for her son, because that makes him almost next of kin.

"What the hell? Where's the fire?" he rasps, and I open my mouth, but instead of saying something I gulp down air and nearly hyperventilate. Drum straightens up and looks annoyed and disgusted. "Oh. Again?"

I nod. "Ambulance," I say, and my voice sounds like I'm a little kid. "Pills," I say, trying to sound normal, but my voice isn't working very well. It's strange. I was fine when I was talking to the ambulance people.

Drum rubs his eyes and swears again. "She's at the hospital?" he asks, and I nod.

Drum curses. He leaves the door open and twists on his heel, striding back inside. I hesitate, then follow.

His place is a mess, but not a dirty mess, just too much junk in too small a space. Lots of music magazines, lots of CDs and even old-fashioned records. His drum set is so big it takes up almost all the space.

Drum's in the bedroom, moving around and still cursing. Then he emerges, still no shirt, but he's wearing his leather jacket and has a duffel bag thrown over his shoulder. He starts when he sees me, like he'd forgotten all about me.

"I'm off, kid," he says, striding toward the door. He shoves a hand through his hair, then puts his hand on the doorknob and pauses, his back to me. "I can't do this anymore. You're on your own."

My heart starts pounding almost as fast as it did

when I first saw Mom lying gray and still. He'd said he'd leave if it happened again. I'd forgotten.

"Please," I say, even though I don't want to beg, and I don't want to sound like a tiny scared kid. "Will you call the hospital?"

Drum still doesn't look at me. He yanks the door open, and I follow him down to the garage. He throws his bag in the trunk, opens the garage door, and slides behind the wheel. "I can't," he says, his jaw clenched. "You're not my kid. Understand? You are not my responsibility, and I can't get myself mixed up in this mess."

I say nothing. I can't think of anything that will convince him, but he pauses, his fingers tapping the steering wheel hard in a rapid rhythm, almost like one of his drum solos. He digs the keys out of his pocket and starts the car. As he puts the car in gear, he looks at me for a split second, then shakes his head and stares into the rearview mirror.

"You'll be fine," he says harshly, still staring into the mirror like he's talking to someone in the backseat. "There's a whole army of people out there whose job it is to help you. They'll do a better job than I ever could. Don't worry. Okay?"

He doesn't let me answer, but backs out of the garage and revs the engine, and the car shoots down the street and vanishes.

The Cadillac goes faster than the ambulance did.

An hour passes, and I just sit on the garage floor and stare at a puddle of oil on the floor and a trail leading out of the garage. There must be a problem with Drum's Cadillac. Cars aren't supposed to leak oil like that.

I don't dare call the hospital myself to check on Mom, because they will want to speak to an adult, and when nobody is here they'll come and take me away, put me in foster care or in an institution, and Mom will be all alone.

A panic attack is trying to overwhelm me, but I fight it. I try to think, try to be logical, define the problem and brainstorm the solutions like I was taught at one of the applied logic workshops Mom sent me to. It worked on logic problems, maybe it will work on this, too.

And it does. The answer comes to me—Mr. Rawls. He's home now. He can call the hospital for me. He will help. I know he will.

I'm over there before I know, off my bike and up on the porch so quickly that my bike is still upright when I ring the bell. I don't want to think, just do, and I try not to think while I tell him everything, how I just need an adult to call the hospital for me, say they're looking after me and need to check on my mom.

"Wait . . . wait . . ." Mr. Rawls holds up his hands. "I don't understand a word you're saying. Come inside." I trail after him into the kitchen, and he has me sit at the table and gives me a glass of water. "Again," he says. "Tell me again. Your mother is at the hospital?"

"Yes," I whisper into my glass, and drink up. My mouth is dry, but I'm nauseous when I've emptied the glass. "I need to know how she is. They won't talk to a kid. I need you to call for me. Tell them you're looking after me, and that way they'll talk to you."

This time Mr. Rawls understands. He writes down my mom's full name and address and picks up the phone without asking any more questions. But he looks at me with pity, and I hate it so much that I leave the room and go look at the aquarium while he makes the call. I've watched the red and yellow fish, my favorite, make two rounds before Mr. Rawls comes and sits down next to me.

"No news yet," he says quietly. "But they promised to call as soon as there is anything to report."

I press the pad of my thumb against the glass where a fish nibbles at a piece of greenery. "Okay."

"Would you feel better waiting at the hospital? We could go there if you'd like."

I shake my head.

Mr. Rawls nods and goes back to the kitchen. He comes back with milk and drops a packet of cookies on the coffee table. I rip it open and stuff a cookie in my mouth despite the nausea. I need something to do with my hands, and sooner or later they'll stop shaking.

Mr. Rawls sits at the other end of the sofa with a cup of steaming coffee. The smell reminds me of Mom, of her smile when she wakes me up in the morning. "Where are your relatives?" he asks. "Your mom—she must have a family somewhere, right?"

I shake my head, glad that I have a cookie in my mouth and can't speak.

"No family? Grandparents?"

"Dead," I tell him when I've swallowed the last crumbs. "No relatives. There's nobody. Just Drum. And he's gone."

"What about your dad, then? He's a big-shot scientist, isn't he? Any way we can track him down?"

"No. How do you know about my dad?"

Nobody's supposed to know. It's a secret, because if everybody knew I was supposed to be a Nobel kid, they would be envious and not approve.

Mr. Rawls smiles and tells me he heard it through the grapevine. I didn't know there was a grapevine about my Nobel dad, just about my mom. If they know, do they believe it at all, the story of my Nobel genes?

Maybe everybody's playing along, pretending, helping Mom keep her world together, gluing the pieces together with lies and fantasies.

Mr. Rawls is still waiting for an answer, and I can't do anything but shrug. I can't tell him the truth. There is no truth. I'm the product of Mom's dream world; anything that shatters her world shatters me.

"You're going to need someone," he says. "This . . . can't go on. You can't live like that. Children shouldn't have to live like that."

"Do you have any kids?" I ask, not expecting an answer, perhaps a shrug only, but maybe it can distract him from reminding me that everything's trouble now.

Mr. Rawls looks at me with a faint smile. "No . . ."

He hesitates, looks away, then at me again, the smile still there. "I have a little one in the cemetery."

It takes me a while to understand what he means. "What happened?"

"She was born too soon. Too small. And then she died." He looks around, and from his movements I can see he wants to reach for a cigarette. I know he quit a while ago, but he still has some of the habits, especially when he needs to find something to do with his hands. I want to ask more questions—I want to know how old his daughter would be now, if she has a name, but I can see that thinking about her upsets him. Even though he's smiling, his hands tremble.

"I'm sorry," I mumble, because I know I'm supposed to, but I don't see the point of saying it. What's he supposed to answer back? That it's okay?

It's not okay. Death is never okay. Mom sometimes tried to tell me it was a natural thing, that everything comes and goes, everything has its time, its place in the cycle of life, but I don't agree.

I want to live forever. I think people should live forever if they want to.

When I still had my Nobel dad, I sometimes wished he was doing research on immortality, but immortality isn't a good idea right now. It would cause problems with overpopulation, because we're not ready for colonizing other planets yet. We're pretty much stuck on planet Earth for now, which means we're stuck with death. So it would have been smarter to wish for a dad who was an astrophysicist or something like that, someone who could help get us into space.

"Yeah," Mr. Rawls says, and I've almost forgotten that we were talking about his dead little girl. "Life happens. And doesn't happen. It isn't always a pretty world we live in, is it?" He taps a finger against the glass of the aquarium and looks at the phone. We're both glancing at the phone every couple of minutes, but it might be a long time before Mom wakes up and they know she's okay.

"Well," Mr. Rawls says at last. "You look exhausted. Would you like to lie down for a while? I've got a guest room that's never been used before."

I shake my head. I'd rather sit here close to the phone. Mr. Rawls nods and makes his cigarette gestures again, looking around randomly. "No problem," he says. "We'll just wait. They'll probably call soon enough."

I don't say anything to that, just stare at the table,

wondering why there are tears in my eyes now, when there weren't before, and I bite my teeth together and try not to blink, because blinking might make the tears fall down, and I just want them to disappear back into my eyes and stay hidden inside forever.

"The aquarium is starting to get dirty again," Mr. Rawls says after a while. He stands up and removes the lid of the tank. He puts his hand in the water, and it looks huge in there. The fish swim around it. One of them nibbles at his finger. I know that tickles, because they've done it to me sometimes. "What do you say we clean it?" Mr. Rawls asks. "We're stuck by the phone for a while anyway. Might as well do something useful."

I don't think the aquarium is dirty. I cleaned it the last time he was away, but he's already disconnecting the heater and gesturing me over.

So I stand up and get the cleaning supplies and the plastic tub for the fish to explore while we work. Cleaning the aquarium takes hours if it's done right.

We make sure we clean it right.

# 10

Mom is in a coma.

This time the drugs had time to go through her stomach and into her blood and everywhere, because it happened in the morning while I was at school and wasn't there to call the ambulance right away. It's bad. She isn't sitting up in the hospital bed, isn't holding out her arms and telling me lies. She's in a coma, and it's all my fault.

The fear is like a snake inside my clothes, sometimes so still I barely know it's there, sometimes squirming and curling around me, tightening around my chest and my stomach, tickling me in unexpected places, the nasty kind of tickle that's agony and you'd do anything to make it go away.

I shake. It's embarrassing, but I can't stop it. My hands shake, my legs shake, even my face seems to shake if I don't work hard at keeping it steady. I keep my hands inside the sleeves of my sweater. That way people maybe can't see it.

Mr. Rawls came with me to the hospital. He waited in a corner of the room and was almost invisible while I sat with my mother, just looking at her, all white and still and hooked up to machines like on TV. She's never been hooked up to machines before. They've always just pumped out her stomach, and then she's been okay.

Mr. Rawls pretended he didn't notice how much I shook, and he got me soda and made me eat a sandwich, which was good because I hadn't eaten anything forever and I was hungry, although I didn't know it. I kept waiting for him to say something stupid to try to comfort me, but he never did, and I was glad.

He talked to the doctors, too. He told them the truth, that he's a neighbor looking out for me because I have no family other than my mom. They looked in the charts and asked about Drum, Mom's boyfriend who's supposed to live with us, the big lie that has saved me until now. Mr. Rawls shrugged and said he was gone. That was enough; they told him everything they wouldn't tell me.

They don't know when Mom will wake up, they don't even know if she'll wake up. She's not so sick that she's dying, either; instead she's stuck somewhere between life and death.

I'm afraid to go to sleep now, knowing Mom may sleep forever in a white hospital bed, never again laugh or cry or scream, but not die, either. Sleeping forever is almost worse than death. I don't want her to die, but I don't want her stuck in between, either. It doesn't seem like a nice place to be.

Mr. Rawls has started to look at me funny, sort of like Drum did, like he's not happy with being involved in this and wants to get rid of me, but only when he thinks I won't notice. I missed school today because we went to the hospital early in the morning, and he came with me into the house when we got home. I didn't ask him; he just walked inside with me like it was normal, and he looked around and saw all the painted doors and the empty paint cans, but he didn't say anything, just asked if I wouldn't like to grab some of my stuff and come stay at his house until my mom was better.

I don't want to leave. I tried to tell him so politely, explaining that I want to stay here, that I always sleep best in my own bed, and he'd be just a couple of houses away; I'd be fine.

I could tell he didn't like leaving me behind, because he's responsible for me now; they've written down his name and everything, and made him sign something. But in the end he said okay and programmed his phone number into our speed-dial. Then he looked in the fridge and said we needed to go shopping, but when he'd filled the fridge and asked again if I was sure I wanted to stay here alone, he finally left.

The night feels different without Mom in the house. I don't have to strain my ears to hear her move around. I don't have to be ready if I hear her go to the bathroom, ready to sneak out there and do my counting. It makes me lonely, and loneliness makes me unable to sleep, and when I suddenly hear a sound in the middle of the night my heart hammers in my chest like there are at least five of them there competing against each other.

Someone must have broken into the house.

First I want to run out of the house screaming, but then I'd have to leave my room and probably run straight into the burglars. Then I want to go out the window, but it creaks when it's opened, and I'm afraid it could take me too long, and they'd get me.

Maybe it's best to wait, not to panic and start screaming, but wait and let them take what they want and leave.

I get out of bed and smooth the covers, to make it look like nobody has slept in this bed, nobody's home. I grab my computer, sitting in its carrier by my bed, and slide under the bed. Dust curls around me until I'm invisible.

I used to hide here from Mom sometimes when I was little, not because she would hurt me, but because when she got high on the pills or the booze, it was like she turned into someone else, almost some*thing* else, and it scared me. Then it happened more and more often, and I got used to it.

Minutes pass. I lie there in the dust, looking up at my bedsprings, and wait for the burglars to go away. I'm not very afraid now; I'm just waiting, but I'm worried about tomorrow. Mr. Rawls isn't going to be happy about this. He probably won't let me stay here alone again if he finds out we were burglarized.

Then I hear Mom's voice, drifting through the air and into my room, calling to me in a gentle, teasing tone, a tone that seems to grab hold of my wrist and softly pull me from under the bed. I stand up and brush the dust off my pajamas as I walk to the door, my bare toes curling on the cold floor, and listen.

She calls again. The voice is coming from the living room, and I walk down the darkened hall.

Mom is home.

She's standing beside the television, her back to me, and when she turns around, she smiles. The coma has stenciled dark circles under her eyes, and she's wearing white hospital pajamas with her hair loose and uncombed, but she's here, and she's smiling.

She beckons for me to come to her, and I do, opening my mouth to ask a million questions, but she stops me, finger against her lips and a conspiratorial wink like when I was little and we still played together. She turns toward the door painted on the wall, reaches for the doorknob, turns it, and pushes the small door open.

I stop, stare at her, stare at the door, the door that isn't real, the door that can't open, and I know this isn't really happening. It's like in the movies when reality is suddenly exposed as a dream. Mom is not okay. She's not home. She's not standing there, smiling at me. She's still in a coma at the hospital, and I'm lying in my bed dreaming, and I want to wake up, turn on the other side, and go back to sleep, because I don't like comforting lies, even in a dream.

Mom holds out her hand and steps toward the open door, bowing her head as she prepares to enter. She waits for me, and the dream won't go away, I won't wake up, so I allow it to continue and take her hand.

Her hand is not cold, like I expected it to be, like it usually is, both at home and at the hospital. It's warm and dry, and she squeezes my hand as if to tell me not to be afraid, before vanishing through the door, one hand trailing behind as she pulls me in after her.

The other side is darkness. My feet are bare, and I shiver, but my mom's hand is emitting warmth to me and that helps.

*Where are we going?* I ask. Because it's a dream I can ask without speaking, and Mom squeezes my hand again, then pulls me forward, and I understand she's going to show me, not tell me.

I follow her through the narrow corridor, feeling cold emanate from the walls. I reach out to touch them, and feel uneven brick on both sides. I smell mildew and something that reminds me of the ocean, but I see nothing; the darkness is complete.

We finally emerge through another low door, and even in a dream I have to squint against the light.

We're in a long hallway, like something from a fantasy castle; the walls are high, with picture portraits lining the walls on both sides. Mom points to the portraits, smiling, and I recognize them; they're the Nobel winners from my book, my Nobel dads, now in color instead of black and white. The portraits are alive, the Nobel dads are watching me, smiling at me, some stern, some teasing, some surprised, but my mom nods gracefully to each one, and I find myself doing the same.

I'm still aware that I'm dreaming, and I've read about this. It's called "lucid dreaming," and when you dream like this you can often control the dream, you can even fly or do whatever you want. I read about it in a science magazine a long time ago, and it sounded so cool. I always wanted to try it, but it never happened until now.

I hold out my arms and take a running leap, trying to fly, but I just stumble over my own feet and clutch at the wall to avoid falling flat on my face. Mom looks at me, surprised, and then she laughs because she can read my mind and knows what I'm trying to do. Then she tells me this is her dream, not mine, and I can only control my own dreams.

I want to know how I ended up in her dream, but she keeps going and doesn't hear that question, or maybe she just doesn't want to answer it.

We reach the end of the corridor. We've nodded at all the Nobel winners, and Mom turns back. This time I notice that doors line the walls, below the pictures. All sorts of doors, and some of them remind me of the doors Mom painted on the walls in our house.

Mom opens some of the doors and peeks in. Most of the doors are small, so I can't see past her and inside, but sometimes there's a draft, sometimes noise, sometimes light, sometimes nothing at all. Mom seems to be looking for something, and I follow and wait. She brought me here, so there must be something she wants to show me.

# 11

Nothing's changed.

It's been days, and Mom is still in a coma at the hospital, and I have dreams about her every night. We always go to the corridor lined with pictures of the Nobel dads, and we look at the doors. Sometimes we just look, and sometimes Mom opens a door and shows me inside. Occasionally she holds the door open for me and lets me pass through, but doesn't come with me. Sometimes we both go through.

This is strange. Nothing in my science magazines explains it, and I'm too logical to believe in paranormal stuff, so I don't know what to think. She shows me people and places, all sorts of things, like they're from her past; it looks most of all like they're her memories. But it can't be. It has to be just my imagination, but it feels very real. Some of it's scary, some is funny, and some of it makes me wake up sad and crying, even as the images fade away as dreams always do. But the dreams don't help me. There's nothing there to help wake Mom out of the coma, nothing that helps me find my dad, but at least I'm with my mom for a while every night.

Whenever I wake up, I always jump straight out of bed and go look at all the doors Mom painted on the walls. There's no point, of course. It's just paint, and none of them is ever open.

Mr. Rawls has spoken to the social workers at the hospital, and they let me stay with him for the time being. I eat dinner at his house, but I sleep at our house. I go to school as usual, then I go to the library and read books and browse websites. I mostly read about comas in case I discover something important the doctors haven't told us. I also read a lot about dreams, but I haven't found out anything new yet, nothing that explains what is happening.

Then in the afternoon I go see Mom. Sometimes Mr. Rawls drives me, but sometimes I ride there on my bike. I've almost got permission to visit on my own. Mr. Rawls talked to one of the nurses, and if I make sure I visit on her shift, she sneaks me in.

Mom still isn't getting better. They say she isn't worse, either, but I think she looks worse. She's thinner, paler, and she seems smaller, like she's shrinking. She looks worse than she does in my dreams, and her hands are always icy.

I read to her from the science magazines every day. They say sometimes people in a coma know when you're there and talking to them, even though they can't respond, can't even move a finger or an eyelid to let you know they're awake. If Mom knows I'm here, I'm sure she'd like me to read to her.

I try to pick the articles I think she'd like best. Yesterday we read about how the universe was created, the Big Bang and black holes and stuff. Cosmology and astrophysics are hard to understand, and when I still thought I had a Nobel dad I was angry at myself for not being able to understand everything about black holes and time travel and the speed of light. Now that I know I'm just normal, it's okay. Most people find these things difficult to understand.

The coolest thing they said in the article was that people were originally made of stardust. All the atoms in our bodies were created in giant supernova explosions billions of years ago, *eons* ago. Then they drifted around space and formed gas clouds and planets and the primordial soup, and eventually stardust became proteins and cells and organisms and dinosaurs and people.

I really like that idea. What's even cooler is that someday my atoms may again start drifting around space. Maybe my atoms will someday be a part of a new star or a new planet, or a new person. Maybe an alien dinosaur. Anything. Being stardust is much cooler than having Nobel genes.

They mentioned the Bible story too. Mom is always telling me to go deeper and read the sources behind the stories, so I brought the Bible with me today and read the story of creation to Mom.

God went about creation in a strange way. He let there be light before he created the sun, for example. Mr. Rawls came with me to the hospital today, and it seemed he hadn't heard the story of Genesis before. He laughed when I came to the end and said obviously God had first created the beasts, then realized they weren't beastly enough, so he created Man.

I guess Mr. Rawls doesn't like people very much, but that's okay. I don't like them much either.

* * * * *

They are there when I come home from school one day, two women, sitting in our kitchen with Mr. Rawls. I instantly know who they are. They look official and they smile too wide, and why else would they be here if not to take me away?

Mr. Rawls said I could stay until Mom woke up. He has betrayed me.

Mr. Rawls sees the look on my face and stands up. I twist around and bolt for the door before they can get me, but as I grapple with the knob, Mr. Rawls catches up with me and puts his hands on my shoulders. "Hey," he says. "It's okay. Don't panic."

"No!" I yell, pulling at the doorknob, kicking the door, but Mr. Rawls reaches out to hold it shut, and he's stronger than I am.

"Listen to me," he says, tightening his hand on my shoulder when I keep hammering at the door. "Listen!"

"Listen to what?" I spit out. "You turned me in. I was doing fine. I could have stayed here until Mom came home, and everything would have been okay again."

"When were things ever okay in this house?" Mr.

Rawls asks quietly, and I squeeze my eyes shut and look down. My hair is getting too long, and I let it fall down over my eyes. I don't want to see him. I don't want him to see me. "Things can't go on like this," he continues. "You know that. Your mom is very sick, and you're still a child. We've gotten away with this for a while, but legally I can't take responsibility for you. You know all this, don't you?" He flips the hair out of my face, but I still refuse to look at him. "You're a smart kid. You have to realize we don't have a choice. Right?"

Smart kid. Right.

I lean back against the door and slide down to sit on the floor. This is my worst fear, and it's finally happening. "I can't leave my mom!" I mean to shout, but it's only a whisper. "I have to visit her. Somebody has to visit her and talk to her and read to her. I can't leave her alone."

Mr. Rawls sits down next to me. "Tell them that. Talk to them. They're not on a mission to take your mom away from you. They're here to help you."

I rest my head on my knees. "What's going to happen?" I whisper.

"I don't know. They think they've found . . ." Mr.

Rawls stands up. He holds out a hand to help me up. "Come on. Let's talk to them."

I stand up without taking his hand and walk ahead of him back to the living room. The social workers are sitting on the couch, but I think they just sat down again. They were probably at the door, watching and listening.

"I can't leave my mom," I tell them as I sit down in the chair farthest away from them. "She's in a coma, and it's important to visit her every day. It's important to talk to her and read to her. The doctors say so. It might help bring her back."

One of the social workers looks rather old, and the other one is my mom's age. They don't answer me. Instead they introduce themselves, and shake my hand, and their smiles are still too wide.

"I can't leave," I repeat. "Mom has nobody except me. I can't leave her."

The younger one clears her throat. "Actually, you do have other family," she says. She stands up from the couch and kneels down on the floor beside my chair, getting down to my level like I'm some little kid. She smiles. "Isn't it great news? We have found your grandparents."

Grandparents.

Grandparents?

I don't have any grandparents.

"Your mother's parents," she clarifies, as if I need to be told that when the place on my birth certificate for the father's name is empty. "Your grandma will be picking you up soon. Isn't it exciting?"

She's talking to me like I'm a baby, and it's pissing me off. Grandparents? I'm dizzy with confusion, but it doesn't change the most important thing: I can't leave my mother.

"I can't leave," I say again. "I have to stay."

The social worker smiles. It's supposed to be a friendly smile, I guess, but to me it's just a grimace, and it tells me nothing I say will make the slightest difference.

"You know your mother is very sick," she says. "Don't you?"

Reluctantly I nod.

"There's been little change in her condition. We don't know when she'll wake up, or if she'll be in any condition to take care of you when she does. Mr. Rawls has been very kind, but you can't stay with him forever. Someone has to take care of you."

Take care of me? I want to shout that it's the other way around, I need to take care of Mom, I *have* to take care of her, I can't leave her behind all alone—but I know better. If they knew I was the one taking care of my mom instead of the other way around, they'd never let me go back to her.

"Mom needs me," I say, even though I know it won't do me any good. "She's sick. I don't want to leave her when she's sick."

The woman keeps smiling. "Don't worry. You're not going far. Your grandparents live just two hours away. Your grandma will be here soon to pick you up. Maybe you should pack your things and be ready?"

Again I think about running away, but I'd be running away from my mom as well, and then there would be no point. I've often thought about running away before, but I don't think I'd actually do it. I know bad things can happen to runaways. It wouldn't be a smart thing to do, but nevertheless I think about it.

It's an option.

Not one I'll use, not now, but somehow it makes me feel better to have options, to imagine the different possibilities. Like there are many doors for me to open instead of just one.

I pull open my closet and stare inside without seeing anything while I think about the possibilities—about my mom and my grandparents and running away. Why did Mom lie to me about my grandparents?

I guess she lied so I would never ask again.

I have grandparents.

*Maybe my grandparents know who my real father is.*

The thought strikes sudden and swift, and I stop breathing until my chest hurts, reminding me I need oxygen to live.

Maybe they know his name and where he lives and everything. Maybe they can give me his address, and I could go meet him.

I get goose bumps all over, and my scalp tickles, as if my hair is standing on end like in comic books.

Maybe I'm just one question away from finding my dad.

The thought is so exciting that energy fills my body. I start yanking clothes off the shelves and stuffing them into a duffel bag. I can't wait to meet them. Can't wait to ask them.

But I will have to wait.

I slow down and start folding my shirts properly, regaining control of myself. The timing must be right. I'll have to get to know them first, so I can tell when they're telling the truth and when they're lying. That's always important when you're asking people questions.

I've read about it, the gestures that give people away when they're lying, their body language. There is flickering of the eyes, the way they touch their face, the way they move their hands, but people don't consciously read these signs. It's instinct that tells you when people aren't being honest; you sort of know without knowing how you know. It's subconscious. And you can't always rely on your instincts. They don't always work correctly, and some people are better at it than others. I think my instincts are getting pretty good. I've had a lot of practice.

I don't know what will happen now, if I'm ever coming back to our house again, so I'm careful not to leave anything behind that I want to see again. I take the photo albums and the important stuff like my birth certificate and other paperwork, stuff Mom has told me is important not to lose. There's my computer, too.

When I'm done, I grab a science magazine and sit down on the living room sofa, sit and read and wait for my grandmother to get here. The older social worker is gone, but the young one is still there, sitting with her clipboard, writing. She smiles at me and asks me a few questions, but then she leaves me alone, and I pretend to concentrate on my magazine.

I don't want to be too excited, but time passes slowly while I wait, and my heart leaps when the doorbell finally rings, and my fingers turn numb, so I drop the magazine. I sit there waiting while the social worker gets the door, and a woman appears in the doorway, staring at me with wide eyes and covering her mouth with her hand.

She looks like Mom.

She isn't as old as I expected. When I pictured my grandmother, it was a typical one from the storybooks for children—white hair, bent back, someone old— but she looks younger than some of my teachers. Her hair isn't even gray. Her face is a lot like Mom's face, especially her eyes. It feels weird to look at her.

She stares at me. Then her mouth trembles in a smile and a hand reaches out toward me, but then she pulls it back and bursts into tears, which is pretty embarrassing, even though they're silent tears with deep gulps of breath, and she's not howling or anything. I don't know what to do, so I just look away.

The social worker pats her shoulder. "Come over here," she says to me, her smile more natural this time. "Meet your grandmother."

I obey, and my grandmother hugs me, carefully, like she's afraid I'll break. It's a long hug, and she smells of flowery perfume, and I start getting claustrophobic, like when Mom hugs me too long, but finally she lets go and her whole face is wet with tears. "How are you?" she whispers. "Oh, you look so much like your mother."

"So do you," I say.

My grandma looks surprised, then laughs. "I heard that a lot when she was a child." She reaches out and touches my face, cups my cheek, runs her hand over my hair. "I never thought I'd get to meet you," she whispers, and I grab the words and hold them in my mind, because they're a *clue*. She said she didn't think she'd ever get to meet me. That means she knew I existed.

How?

Later I'll ask.

"Have you seen my mom?" I ask her. That's important.

"Not yet," Grandma says. "I thought we'd visit her together on our way home." She touches my face again, and I try to keep still. She's taking me to see Mom. She's not taking me away from Mom, not forbidding me to visit. "I'm so happy to have found you," she says again, her voice hoarse. "Both of you."

The social worker clears her throat. "Always wonderful to witness family reunions," she says. She pulls out some documents from her clipboard. "I just need a few signatures, and then I'll leave you two to get acquainted."

My grandmother signs some documents and they talk for a while, sometimes in whispers I'm not supposed to hear, but I don't care anyway. Then the social worker shakes my hand, tells me she'll come visit us next week, and leaves.

We're alone in the house, and my grandmother is again staring at me like I'm something brand-new in the world, something nobody's ever seen before, a newborn.

"I'm all packed," I say, gesturing to my two duffel bags. Now that it's inevitable that I'm leaving, I just want to go, get it over with, see what happens, and then decide what to do next.

"I'd like to look around the house first. If I may?" my grandmother asks, and I'm surprised she waits for my permission. I nod, even though I don't want anyone at all snooping through our things. She walks through the house slowly, her mouth slightly open and her gaze settling on every object in the room, but she doesn't mess with anything.

The house doesn't look so bad now. I cleaned up, and now that Mom isn't here while I'm at school, it stays pretty neat and there aren't overflowing ashtrays everywhere. The only thing that looks weird are all the painted doors, and my grandmother stares at them for a long time but doesn't say anything. Then she looks at our bookshelves.

We have hundreds of books and magazines, mostly science and nature, but quite a lot of literature, too. My grandmother looks impressed, and suddenly I'm proud of my mom.

"She always liked to read," my grandmother whispers as she strokes a finger over the spine of the books. "She was smart. Is," she corrects herself. "Your mother is a very bright girl. She always did well in school. We thought she would go to college and become a doctor or a scientist. She was so interested in such things, so ambitious. . . ." She shakes her head. "Well, plenty of time to talk later."

"Do we go see Mom now?" I ask. I'm wondering what to call her. She didn't tell me her name. I don't even know my grandmother's name. Do I call her Grandma?

My grandmother nods. "Yes. I wanted to pick you up first, so you could introduce the two of us. Tell her I'm here. I know she won't hear us, but still—"

"She might hear," I say. "Sometimes people in a coma know what's going on around them."

"Yes. It's been such a long time since I saw her. . . . I would like you to be there too."

She's nervous about seeing Mom, and I don't blame her. The coma has done strange things to Mom's face. Sometimes she seems like a stranger as she lies there so still. Sometimes she seems dead.

My grandmother starts crying when she sees Mom, so after I tell Mom she's there, I flee into the corridor. I left magazines on Mom's table, in case someone takes the time to read to her while I'm away. If she wakes up, she'll be glad to find the magazines, and she'll know who brought them, even though I'm not there.

I find an old tabloid abandoned on a windowsill and slide down on the floor in a corner, pretending to read it. It's junk, but reading junk is better than staying in there and watching my grandmother cry silently while Mom just lies there and may not even know her own mom has found her again.

I start wondering if Mom will be happy about it when she wakes up. My grandmother seems nice enough, but there must be a reason why Mom told me she was dead. Maybe I can find out now. Maybe my grandmother has a lot of puzzle pieces that I've been missing, maybe she knows about my dad, and maybe she knows stuff about my mom that I never knew before.

I guess I'll be going to a new school now. New kids, new teacher, new everything. I wonder if everybody there will automatically know about Mom and all. It's strange how news like that travels.

I turn the thin, crackling pages of the tabloid and think about lies and truths. I hope my grandmother doesn't also believe the Nobel lie, because if she does, she won't be able to help me find out the truth.

# 12

After the hospital visit, we drive to my grandparents' house. My grandmother has a cool car. It's a big silver-gray Mercedes; it must have cost a fortune. The inside smells of leather, like it's brand-new. It couldn't be more different from Drum's beat-up old Cadillac, but it still reminds me of Drum.

I've heard a lot of the kids complain that their grandmothers are horrible drivers, inching along on the highway. Mine isn't like that, but she drives precisely at the speed limit; the meter doesn't dare climb even a fraction of an inch over it.

We don't talk a lot during the two-hour drive, but I like just sitting quietly watching the view and thinking. My grandmother tries to start a conversation a few times, but I get the feeling she's not used to talking to kids. She doesn't seem to know what to say except to ask about school, and there isn't all that much to say about school.

I've never been this far away from home before, and there are fewer and fewer houses, and then the last suburbs fade into farmland and a distant horizon. It looks weird, like I'm watching it on television.

Then we're in a kind of suburb again, and finally we drive up to a big house. It's practically a mansion, and I just stare at it. The house has columns, like the Greek temples in my history books, and there are about a million big windows. The grounds are huge too, grass and flowerbeds and big, ancient trees.

I wonder if they're fruit trees. I've always wanted to pick a fruit off a tree and eat it, like people did before there were towns and cities and jobs and civilization, and the only job was finding shelter and enough to eat. Everything's so complicated now, and nobody eats fruit directly off the trees.

"Wow," I whisper as we stop in front of the big house. I don't mean to say it out loud, but Grandma smiles and ruffles my hair, like she's glad I'm impressed. I don't like her ruffling my hair like Mom used to do, but I don't dislike it either. It's something you do to little kids and I'm getting too big for it, but it's okay, I guess.

"The house may be big," she says. "But it's been empty. I lost my treasure many years ago, but I hope I won't lose either of you again."

I want to make a face, because calling me and Mom a treasure seems silly, but I don't. I'm trying to be polite, a good reflection of Mom. She would want me to.

A curtain moves in one of the upper windows, and someone is there, wearing all white, reminding me of the nurses in Mom's hospital.

"One thing I should tell you before we go in. It's about your grandfather . . . he's not well." She pulls the keys from the ignition and puts them in her purse, then sighs. "He's had strokes. . . . Do you know what a stroke is?"

I nod, and Grandma smiles, almost like Mom does when she's happy with me. "Well, he's not doing very well. He's not going to be able to talk to you, but he understands everything. Please don't be afraid to talk to him. He'll be happy to see you."

She starts whispering, and it's just like Mom does, she whispers to hide the tears in her voice. "We're so happy to have a grandson. You're our only grandchild, you know." She wrestles a tissue from her purse and blows her nose, and her voice is normal again.

"Sure," I say. It's okay. I know a lot of kids are scared of sick people, but I don't mind. Talking to my grandfather won't be that different from spending time with my mother lying in the hospital bed, stuck inside her coma.

Maybe I can read to my grandfather like I read to my mom. Maybe he likes science magazines too. At least my grandfather would be awake to hear me read, while I never know if my mom hears me at all.

I crane my neck in all directions when we enter the house. I'm curious about everything, but I don't get to explore now. Grandma takes me right upstairs to meet my grandfather.

My grandfather is lying in a hospital bed in a large room that looks like it wasn't always a bedroom. He's very thin and looks small, although I can see by the length of his legs under the blankets that he is a tall man.

He struggles to raise his head when he sees me, but even that fails. I walk to him and take his hand, shake it like normal and say hello, just as if he were okay, just as if he'd extended his hand and greeted me first. I'm good at pretending such things.

He stares at me, one eye alive, the other hooded, and his hand is cold and clammy.

"You're our only grandson," my grandmother whispers. She told me this just a moment ago, and I get the feeling that this time she's talking for my grandfather. "We're so glad we finally got to meet you. I thought about you every day. Every day. Didn't we, dear?"

My grandfather moves a finger, and my grandmother smiles. "See?" she tells me. "Once for yes, twice for no. It's amazing how far that will get you."

My grandfather gets tired easily, so we don't stay in his room for long. When both his eyes start to close, we leave him to rest. My grandma has tears in her eyes again, and she tells me how much it meant to my grandfather to see me, but I don't know how she could tell. He couldn't do anything but just look at me.

She shows me the house, and it doesn't seem quite as big on the inside as it did when I saw it from the car. All the rooms are really big, but there aren't that many of them. Old furniture takes up a lot of space, and large paintings decorate the walls in almost every room. I look at them with a bit of envy. I always wanted to paint on a huge canvas like that, but they didn't have them at school.

I get my own room, and it's as big as our living

room at home. It feels empty, though. There's a huge bed, and lots of closets, and a desk, and a big bookshelf filled with literature, but there's so much space that the room still seems empty. My grandmother said something about getting me better furniture, but I don't want that. I'm not staying here for long. Mom will get better soon, and we'll go home.

But maybe we could visit here sometime now that I have real grandparents like most other kids. We could visit, and I could read to Grandpa.

I have my own bathroom, too. It's the size of my bedroom back home, and there's a big tub as well as a shower. Mom would love this. She loves taking long baths with lots and lots of soap and bubbles, so the whole house smells of lavender for a long time, but she always complains that our bathtub is too small. Maybe that's because she was used to this kind of bathroom when she was little and still lived with her parents.

Dinner is really fancy, with candles and crystal glasses, even though it's just the two of us. My grandparents have a cook, so Grandma doesn't need to cook and I don't have to set the table. The cook made my favorite meal, chicken in curry, and it's nice, but it tastes different from when Mom or I cook it.

Grandma and I talk over dinner. Or rather, she talks. I just eat and nod and listen very carefully for clues. Later I'll sneak in all the important questions, but now I'm gathering information and she's telling me all sorts of stuff. Some of it from long ago, when Mom was a little girl, and some of it more recent, like about my grandpa's strokes. It's all jumbled together and disorganized, and I don't always follow what she means, but I try to remember it all. I like listening to her talk about my mother as a little girl, even though it feels like she's talking about someone else.

"Do we visit Mom tomorrow?" I ask, interrupting her. Grandma puts down her fork and adjusts her napkin.

"Not tomorrow," she says, and my stomach tightens. "But the day after. Okay? Tomorrow we need to get you settled. We need to deal with a lot of paperwork. And find you a school."

I put down my own fork. Clench my hands. "I have to visit Mom every day."

"Yes. And you will, soon. I wish we could take her home, but she needs hospital care. There's a private hospital close by. I hope to have her moved there as soon as possible."

The knot inside loosens so suddenly that I let out a huge sigh of relief.

Mom will be close by.

I have grandparents.

Mr. Rawls was right. This is for the best.

I looked forward to the first night in my new room in my grandparents' house, sleeping in a new bed and meeting my mom in my dreams and telling her about Grandma. But she didn't come to me. Not the first night, and not after that. My dreams are just random flashes and weird stuff like they always were. Mom isn't there anymore, and I miss her.

The days pass. They always do. Mom moves to the new hospital close by, in a nice private room with a view and a television and a stereo, and I'm allowed to visit whenever I want. I bring her music and leave something playing when I have to go. We're also listening to *East of Eden* on audiobook. I've never read it, but I found the book on a shelf in my new room. Mom's name was in it, and there was a bookmark about halfway through, so maybe she didn't finish it before she left. I thought she'd like to know how it ended, so I got her the audiobook.

But she doesn't wake up.

Grandma didn't mention school again for a few days, and when I finally asked her, because Mom always says I must be careful not to fall behind, she looked surprised, like she'd forgotten. Then she said she would look into it, and added that it's probably best I take a few days to settle in, and start school next week.

Maybe school is more complicated for rich people. Maybe she'll send me to a private school, where I'll have to wear a uniform and a tie. Mom would laugh if she saw me wearing a tie.

I don't mind not starting school until next week. I go to the hospital in the morning and stay there for hours, reading and playing music, even doing puzzles or playing solitaire while talking with Mom.

Then I go home to the mansion, and I spend a lot of time with my grandfather. He can't talk, or do anything, but I don't mind. He's still my grandfather, and I've never had one before. I read to him, or we watch movies together, and sometimes I just chat, like I do with Mom. It's strange how I'm much better at chatting with Mom and Grandpa, when they're the only people who can't say anything back.

It's hard to know what Grandpa is thinking, even

though I can ask him yes and no questions, but I think he likes it that I hang around. He likes the science magazines best, just like Mom. At least he keeps his eye open and doesn't fall asleep as much as when I read storybooks or the newspapers.

When my grandfather is tired and needs to rest, I do other stuff. Sometimes I play on the computer or read or explore the neighborhood on the new bike Grandma bought me. There's plenty to do, so sometimes I worry I won't have enough time once I'm back at school.

Even though Mom hasn't woken up I'm happy, because she has all those expensive doctors to take care of her and I'm sure they'll cure her soon. Maybe this time things will be different when she wakes up. Maybe she'll be happy. Maybe she won't go back to the pills and booze now that she has her own mom and dad again.

Maybe we can live with them in the mansion instead of going back to our little house. At least for a while. Maybe I'll never again have to count pills or stay up all night listening at the door.

*   *   *   *

Then one day as I sit with Mom, reading to her from *National Geographic*, one of the doctors comes and asks Grandma to follow him.

My grandmother looks older when she comes back, and I stop reading and jump to my feet because she looks like something bad has happened. She puts her arm around me, hugging me. She isn't very big, we're the same size, a few more months and I'll probably be taller than her. I can tell something's wrong.

"What is it, Grandma?" I ask, my voice showing how worried I am.

Grandma shakes her head. She stares at the machines hooked up to my mother, then at her, and back at the machines.

"What's wrong?" I ask again, and Grandma takes my hand, squeezes it. "What did they say?" I get scared when she doesn't answer. "Is Mom going to die?" I ask at last, my voice hoarse in desperation.

"No . . . but . . . they say . . . they say . . ." Grandma pauses. She holds both my hands tightly. "They don't see any improvement, and apparently, at this stage that means her condition is unlikely to change."

"That she'll never . . ."

"The longer she stays like this, the worse it looks.

They're afraid she'll never wake up." Tears start rolling down Grandma's cheeks. She drops my hands and picks up my mother's hand instead. "Baby," she whispers, leaning over my mother, and tears drop on Mom's sheets. "Please. Please wake up."

As Grandma drives away from the hospital, everything is painfully quiet apart from my loud breathing. It seems my thoughts tumble around inside my head, trying to think of a way to save my mom. I go to Grandpa's room when we get back, and I pretend everything is normal and start reading to him, but I can't concentrate and keep missing lines, reading words wrong, so I give up. I put the book away and start talking instead.

I tell him about Mom, how she just lies there and doesn't move, how her eyes never open, how she's still and quiet like something not alive; how her hands are cold, but her face warm; how white her skin looks even against the stark white hospital sheets.

I don't tell him about the machines that are necessary to keep her alive, and how she might never wake up again. It can't happen, and if I don't talk about it, maybe it won't.

I want to tell Grandpa about the dreams I used to

have, tell him how much I miss seeing my mom in my dreams, but I don't. It's private, just between me and Mom, and I don't want to tell anyone. Not even Grandpa. Not yet.

That evening I ask my grandmother how come they're so rich. I hope it's not a rude question. I'm curious, and I want to think about something other than Mom because my head is starting to hurt from the worry.

Money is interesting. Some people work hard and are lucky and gradually make more and more money, while others work just as hard, but aren't as lucky and never make much at all.

Some people are rich because their family has always been rich, and the kids inherit their parents' money, and later leave their money to their kids, and so on.

It seems logical the money would run out when many generations spend it, but it doesn't. That's because when you have a lot of money, you can use it to make even more money. That's economics, and economics seem even more complicated than calculus, because the rules keep changing.

Grandma looks surprised when I ask. She smiles

and tells me they're not *that* rich, but with the big house and the cool cars and the nurses for Grandpa and staff that works both inside the house and outside, I find that hard to believe.

Then she points at the old paintings on the walls and tells me my grandfather painted them, that he painted almost all the paintings they have on their walls. She says he was a famous artist, and his paintings still sell for a lot of money. "These are worth a lot," she says proudly.

I'm impressed. It's so cool when you can create something out of nothing, and people will buy it for a lot of money. It's almost as if the inside of you is worth something. I'd looked at the paintings a lot, but I never noticed my grandfather's signature in the corner.

I think about Mom's painted doors, and the praise I got from my art teacher. That's where Mom and I got our artistic genes. From Grandpa.

It's a warm feeling inside, like my question marks are filling up with something real and important.

I go upstairs after dinner and sit with Grandpa for a while. We watch TV. I wish he could talk, but the best he can do is make yes or no signs with his hand,

and sometimes even that's too difficult for him. But I tell him I like his paintings.

Grandma comes into the room, and she bends over Grandpa, whispering something in his ear. He makes a sign with his finger, and she nods at him, smiling, and gestures for me to follow her.

She takes me to a door at the end of the hall and opens it with a key. We walk inside darkness, and then Grandma flips the light switch.

The room is large, and the windows are huge. The air smells of paint.

It's Grandpa's studio.

"Nobody's been here in a while," she whispers, and the room echoes the words back at us. "But since you're so interested in your grandfather's work . . ."

Canvases are stacked against the walls, and there's a half-painted canvas on an easel, like my grandfather just put down the brush for a coffee break. The floor is splattered with paint, especially around the easel.

Grandma pats me on the shoulder. "Look around all you like," she says, and leaves, and I think she's crying because the studio is empty without my grandfather there.

Cabinets line one wall, low, below the windows.

There's paint everywhere, tubes and tubes of paint. They sit on top of the cabinets and inside on shelves, and brushes lie on the counter and on a desk in a corner. There's even a small pile of used paints, brushes, and rags under the desk. There's a chair at the desk, and artists' smocks are piled on top of it. They don't look much different from the smocks we wear in art class.

The idea is born as I stand in front of my grandfather's last canvas and stare at the half-formed picture, trying to see what he intended to make of it.

I open a cabinet and take out a few paint tubes, read the labels to find out the colors. There are a lot of colors. I can pick and choose. In a drawer I find fresh brushes that have never been used.

Grandpa has everything I need.

# 13

The door I paint on the wall in my bedroom is my mother's favorite happy color, orange. I play around with the paint, mixing colors to make new ones, and I trim the door with yellow, painting the doorknobs and hinges in deep gold.

I'm not as good at this as my mother is, especially not with the delicate trimming and the pattern of the hinges, but I'm pretty happy with the results. The door may creak, it may squeak, but that's okay, if it opens tonight after I fall asleep.

It doesn't work. It doesn't open to reveal my mom standing there, beckoning me to walk through. All through the night I stare at it, not sure if I'm asleep or not, but it doesn't open.

Finally I get out of bed. My feet sink into the deep carpet, but my toes curl anyway, used to the cold floors at home. I walk to the door and reach out, and the doorknob moves as I touch it—no longer paint, but metal—and the door opens.

I step inside the dark corridor, and it's the same one as before—it feels the same, anyway, only more creepy and scary because I'm alone and not holding on to my mom's warm hand. I feel my way along the brick walls until I find another door, a small one, and crawl out of it.

I've made it. I'm in the huge hall with the pictures of the Nobel dads, and my mom is there, wandering around, looking small and lost and alone.

I run to her and hug her and she smiles, glad to see me, happy and surprised, but nevertheless there is sadness in her eyes.

I wonder if she knows what has happened, if she knows about my grandparents and the new hospital. In my head I ask her everything at once, and she frowns and laughs at the jumble it makes, then smiles mysteriously and makes a gesture meaning to be patient, I'll find out everything in time.

I wait for her to start walking down the corridor like she always does, leading me from door to door and showing me stuff, but she doesn't. She just stands there like we're waiting for something.

Finally I ask her, in our usual silent way, what we're waiting for, and she reaches out and touches my hair and looks sad as she tells me this is *my* dream. I'm in control now. I will choose the doors.

I'm not sure what to do, but I start walking down the corridor. I approach one door, and my mother backs away, shaking her head, then nodding, as if to say she doesn't want to go there, but if that's what I want, I should open the door, because this is my dream.

I don't make her go through the door she doesn't like. I walk on and find another door. This time Mom smiles, and I unlock the door and open it. It's a small door; it reaches only up to my waist, and Mom kneels down and crawls through it.

I follow, and we emerge in a room I've never seen before, but it still looks familiar. It's a girl's room, a rich girl's room, large and filled with toys and stuffed animals and books and even a piano. When Mom smiles and spins around, I know this is her room from when she was little, and I look around with curiosity.

The window is half-open, and outside is the crown of a blooming tree. It's spring, and several birds sit on the branches. Soft wind moves the white curtains with yellow flowers on them, and there are cut tulips in a vase on the windowsill.

I look out the window and I see more trees, more grass, a huge lawn.

It looks familiar.

The trees are taller now, and the faraway house is a different color, but otherwise it looks the same.

My room was once my mom's room. Grandma never told me that.

The next few nights I see more things from when Mom was a little girl. I see her playing in the garden and standing on tiptoe to look up at Grandpa's easel. I try to talk to her about the hospital and the coma, how she needs to wake up so she won't die, but she doesn't hear me. She just waits for me to take her to the doors, so in the end I always do.

When I visit her at the hospital, she just seems paler and paler every day. I hope it's just my imagination, but it feels like she's fading into the white sheets. I'm afraid. It's getting hard to sit with her and read to her, hard to look away from her face and down on the page, because she might die when I'm not looking.

My grandmother doesn't mention the door I painted on the wall in my room, but she is very silent over dinner the next day. A couple of days later there is a big stack of canvases and two easels of different sizes in my room, and a box filled with some of Grandpa's paints. I guess that's a hint.

The day before I start school again, I finally get up the nerve to ask my grandmother the question that's been bouncing around in my head nonstop since I first met her. I've been preparing that question, asking it in a million ways in my head, but in the end I just blurt it out over dinner when we're talking about my old school, not in context with anything at all.

"Do you know who my father is?"

She stares at me for a long time, and I get a sinking feeling, wondering if she, too, thinks I'm a Nobel kid, but then she shakes her head slowly. "I'm sorry. No."

I think she's telling the truth. Maybe she could guess instead. Maybe she knows someone who knows something. I don't say anything, but Grandma keeps looking at me and sees the next question in my eyes. She shakes her head again. "I'm sorry. I have no theories at all. No idea. I never found out."

"I want to find my father. I need to find him."

"I'm sure you do," Grandma says, and leans back in her chair, looking old all of a sudden. She rubs her eyes like she's very tired. "But your mother is the only person who can tell you about him."

My question starts my grandmother talking, answering a lot of other questions I've wanted to ask. She tells me how Mom left home, ran away her junior year in high school and never came back. She tells me how worried she was about my mom, frantic with a biting fear that never lessened, but in time became a constant in life, a part of getting up in the morning and going to sleep at night, a part of everything in between.

Then years later a private detective found her, her and me, and that was the first time they knew I existed, the first time they realized that I must have been the reason she ran away.

My grandmother starts crying again when she talks about the picture the detective brought them, of me around three years old, playing in a sandbox, and my mom sitting on the edge—just a kid herself, Grandma says—reading a book out loud to me.

"She wouldn't talk to us," Grandma whispers. "She wouldn't open the door when I came to visit, she hung up the phone. I don't know why she ran away. Sure, we might have been upset at first that she was pregnant and alone, and so young, but we would have gotten over it. We'd have loved you, we'd have taken care of both of you if only she'd stayed." She gets out a tissue and blows her nose. "When she refused to talk to us, we talked to neighbors, and they said they worried about her and her little one, and we talked to Social Services, and they looked into it, but then they said you were well taken care of, and she was a legal adult by then, so we couldn't force her to come home."

I want to ask more questions, and it feels like there are a lot of them in my head, but somehow I can't think of anything specific to say. It's okay, though. Grandma keeps talking.

"In the end I stopped trying," she says, drying her tears, looking tougher now, almost angry. "You can't make people love you. Not even your children. Especially not your children."

She looks at me with my mother's eyes. "The doctors tell me she's been in trouble for a long time. It must have been hard on you. I'm sorry. I wish I could have been there for you. Both of you."

I shrug. Even though I wanted to know everything,

suddenly I want to go away and not talk about this. But I sit tight, because this is information I need.

"We sent money, every month," Grandma whispers. "And we paid her medical insurance. Your grandfather did. I didn't know about it until he had his stroke two years ago and I started taking care of the finances. I never knew. I wouldn't have thought she'd accept our money, but naturally I kept sending it. I even tried calling her again, to tell her that her father was very ill, that he might be dying . . . but she hung up the phone and still wouldn't talk to me, and then she changed her number."

I remember that. It happened maybe two years ago. Mom told me we changed our number to avoid telephone salesmen.

Grandma shakes her head. "Your mother was a very sick woman, wasn't she?"

She's saying "was," she's using the past tense, and something squeezes my lungs so I can't breathe. She's thinking about the life support machines again.

I have to reach my mom. I have to.

When night falls, I'm again with my mom in the hall with the Nobel pictures and the doors, and I've made up my mind. I head for one of the doors she always shakes her head at, the small dark door almost invisible in the wall underneath the Nobel dad paintings.

Mom has told me this is *my* dream, that I'm in control, and even though she winces and wraps her arms around herself when she sees what I'm about to do, I reach out, undo the lock, and yank the door wide open.

When I turn around to tell my mom we're going inside, she's standing there, staring at me with wide eyes, filled with surprise and hurt and fear like I've never seen.

I don't have a choice. I have to reach my mom, and this is the only thing I haven't tried yet. I get on my knees and crawl quickly through the door, and my mother follows me.

We're in Grandma's house again, my mom's room again, sunny, empty, and I'm disappointed. I thought we would be seeing something new.

I turn toward my mother, remembering that this is my dream, my control. I want to ask about my father, hoping that this dream version of my mother can answer questions without running toward death with her arms open, but when I form the question in my mind, she doesn't reply. She's staring at the bed with her features frozen.

Her bed is big and white, her princess bed with a canopy and many colorful pillows, but there's nothing to see there. I take a step toward my mother, but she holds up a hand and keeps staring, and eventually I start staring too.

Shadows appear, superimposed on the white bed-clothes, and as they become more solid I see my mother, a teenage girl, her face white and frozen, and I see a man, he looks familiar, but I don't recognize him until I hear murmurs of what he says and I hear her call him Daddy, and when I realize what is happening I grab hold of my mother's arm and yank her back, break her gaze, and the shadows disappear.

Mom looks at me, darkness framing her eyes, sadness and grief, and her mouth moves to phrase *I'm sorry*, and this Mom cares about *me*, she's sorry this is causing *me* pain, sorry that I've lost my Nobel dad, because a nonexistent Nobel dad is so much better than the horrible truth.

# 14

I wake up hyperventilating, the panic attack starting even before I wake up, and then before my breathing is even under control I'm in my bathroom because I'm retching and I can't stop, I don't *want* to stop. I want to throw up until there is nothing left to get rid of, like I can dissolve myself from the inside out.

I scratch at my arms and my stomach and my thighs, like I can scrape away the layers until I'm gone. I want to erase myself from the universe. My thoughts aren't thoughts, just emotion and instincts: I shouldn't be here, I don't belong, I should never have come into being.

I'm not crying, but I'm making a sound, a low whine that I hear from outside, something that sounds like it's coming from a hurt animal, and I can't make it stop, until finally I lose consciousness.

*　　*　　*　　*

Again the dream takes me to my mother's bedroom. From the window of my mom's room I can see the windows of another house through the bare branches of the trees. It's winter in this dream. Rain limps down the glass, and through my reflection I see the light in a window, and I remember one of my mother's memories, a memory of sitting in the windowsill staring out at the light and hoping someone would appear in the window, someone would smile and wave and she could let them know she was a prisoner and be rescued by someone who would always take care of her.

I sense Mom smiling wistfully at the memory, and she's there with me, her arms folded over her chest, but she's shivering in her white nightgown, and her hair is wet like she just came in out of the rain. She sits down in the basket chair in the corner and draws her knees up, folding the nightgown over her bare feet. She rests her head on her knees and still shivers. She's cold. She's always cold.

I know Mom isn't really here, she's really lying in her hospital bed, but I still want to help her get warm. I fetch a blanket off the bed and drape it over her shoulders, then kneel down to look into her face. She's pale, and when I touch her hair it's wet, and she looks like the kid Grandma talks about.

"Why's your hair wet?" I ask her, not expecting an answer, but she mutters something lost in the chattering of her teeth.

"So cold," she says, speaking out loud for the first time in my dream. It's her voice, but yet not, it's a young and fragile voice, so thin it breaks apart. "So cold."

"I know. You're always cold."

She doesn't say anything more, and eventually I fade away like I always do when waking up from a dream, leaving her there in the chair, huddling under the blanket, alone.

When I wake up I find the red furrows my nails dug in my skin already struggling to heal, and the revulsion fades a little. My body thinks everything is normal. It's doing its job, sending cells through the bloodstream and pumping out chemicals, trying to fix what's wrong. It doesn't know that *everything* is wrong, that *I'm* wrong, and that it's impossible to fix it. It doesn't know that my mother was right when she said I should aspire to be more than me.

*Just a dream*, some part of me whispers. A dream doesn't mean it's true. It might be just something crazy my head made up.

But it feels true. It explains everything. It explains why Mom told me they were dead and why she ran away to have me, why Grandma can't even guess who my father is. It explains why Mom lied to me about the Nobel dads, why she *had* to lie, and why she had to believe her own lie. There are many clues, and they all fit together.

It takes a long time to get dressed because my body feels weak and my hands shake. I don't take anything with me except my money and my house keys. When I walk down the hall and pass the door to our father's bedroom, I shudder with horror.

I sneak out of the house. Getting home is easier than I thought. I walk a bit, then take a bus, and then another bus, and a couple of hours later I'm back home, I'm putting my key in the lock and opening the door, almost expecting Mom's cigarette smoke to greet me, but of course the house is dark and empty.

Rhythmic sounds reverberate from the garage, slow

and depressive. Drum is back. My heart starts chasing his rhythm, and my footsteps do too. I walk to the bathroom and open both the cabinets. A lot of Mom's pills are still there.

I stare at the bottles. Some of the labels look old, some new. I read them all twice. Then I just look at them, for a long time, until I reach out and my hand hovers over one of the bottles.

I snatch it back.

Anxiety grips me, envelops me like an unexpected wave in the ocean, and I just hold on, wait for it to recede. I know from experience it will, although when I'm submerged it feels like it will never end, like I will be a frozen statue forever, bound by terror of what might happen but still hasn't. When my heart pounds faster and faster and I know I'm diving into another panic attack, I just sink to the floor and try not to think, try to simply let the wave take me, knowing that it will eventually hurl me back—and I will be alive.

When I can move again I go to the kitchen, sit down at the table, and rest my head in my hands. I need to think, if only my thoughts would cooperate. Instead I feel like painful fireworks are exploding inside my skull every time I try to think.

I don't notice that the drumming has stopped until a shadow appears in the doorway, but I don't even jump when he suddenly speaks, because my nerves are just too tired to react.

"What's going on?" Drum asks, our spare key dangling from his hand. "What are you doing back here?"

He doesn't wait for an answer, but picks up the phone. He grabs my arm when I shoot past him, trying to make a run for it. I don't even try to break free. I'm too tired to fight. "Fine," I say. "Call the police."

He doesn't. He flips through our speed-dial instead, and the names show up on the screen. Just as I fear he's going to call the first speed-dial number—911—he moves past it and stops on Mr. Rawls's name instead.

"Come over. The kid is back," he barks into the phone, then hangs up and looks at me. "Promise not to run if I let go?"

Instead of answering I yank my arm back and he lets go, crosses his arms on his chest, and leans back against the wall. "What's going on? Why are you back?"

I open my mouth and words spill out. I don't tell him about our father, but I tell him what happened while he was away, about Mom, the coma, the hospital, Mr. Rawls and then my grandmother, and he nods through it all, like he's following, but I'm not sure he is because it all comes out of my mouth rather a mess, and I haven't finished when Mr. Rawls arrives.

Drum moves away to stand at a distance, gesturing at Mr. Rawls to take over. Mr. Rawls frowns when he sees me, like he hadn't quite believed it when Drum said I was back. He doesn't even have to ask me anything. The words just keep coming, tumbling out of my mouth. I don't tell them about the dreams, because then they'd think I was just imagining things. I tell them everything I found out, stumbling over the words because I hardly know the right ones and they feel dirty in my mouth, but they need to get out.

Mr. Rawls sits there and listens, really listens, and Drum stands at the wall, and he's listening too. When I'm out of words, the silence bangs at my eardrums, and I sit down at the kitchen table, clenching my fists until it hurts.

Drum swears. He pushes himself away from the wall. "I'll be in the garage," he mutters as he leaves the house.

Mr. Rawls sighs. He takes my hands and makes me unclench them, then puts them on the table. I stare at my hands. They feel alien now. All of me does.

"Are you sure you have your facts straight?" Mr. Rawls asks after a while. "Does your grandmother know about this?"

I shake my head, then shrug. I don't know. I don't know anything anymore.

"What can I do?" I whisper, although I feel stupid asking. How can Mr. Rawls give me advice? How could anybody give me advice? There is nothing I can do.

"What do you want to do?"

I want to do what I once saw my Nobel dad do in a dream—I want to yank out the dirty genes, all the bad stuff, so it's not a part of me anymore. I want to be clean, but there's no plastic tub big enough for me now, not enough soap in the universe.

"If this is true, there's nothing you can do about it. It just is. And when there's nothing you can do, you just have to decide it doesn't matter," Mr. Rawls says. "It may matter, but if you decide it doesn't, maybe in time it won't. You know?"

"I can't be . . . this. I can't be me." I'm still choking on the words. Maybe that's why the chemicals in Mom's brain got all scrambled, because she couldn't stand being herself. Maybe she feels all the time like I feel now.

"It's not going to help anyone if you steal your mother's pills and end up in a coma yourself," Drum's voice booms from the doorway. He didn't leave after all. I look up so quickly that I give myself away. They are both watching me. I shake my head, answering a question they haven't asked yet.

How does he know I'd looked like that at Mom's pills? All I did was *look*.

Mr. Rawls stands up. He goes to the bathroom, and I hear the sound of pillboxes and bottles being thrown on top of one another.

"They'll come looking for you soon, kid," Drum says. "You know this is the first place they'll look when they realize you've run away. Where are you going?"

I don't know. I had to leave, I had to come home, but I have no idea what I'm going to do.

"What are you doing back?" I finally think of asking. I thought Drum had left for good.

Drum shrugs. "I didn't go far. I left all my gear behind. And my band is here. I was at a motel. Then I heard you'd both gone and there was nobody to watch the place, so I came back."

There is silence for a while. I'm thinking, but I'm

not thinking—random thoughts float around my brain, but they don't make much sense because they're so disorganized. Mr. Rawls reemerges at last, carrying a paper bag. I hear the sound of the pills tumbling inside the plastic containers when he puts the bag on the floor and sits by my side again.

"Call your grandmother," he suggests, reaching for the phone. "Just tell her you're here, that you got homesick."

I shake my head. It's instinctive. I had to get out of that house. Phoning there is almost like going back.

"If you don't let her know where you are, she'll call the police. If you're labeled a runaway, things will get even more complicated." Mr. Rawls rubs his face with his hands. "More complications is one thing we don't need, right?"

He's right. I pick up the phone and call the house where my grandmother lives, the house where I was created, and I tell her I'm at home, and I'm okay, and that Mr. Rawls is here with me. Grandma is shocked at first. Then she's angry, then sad, and then worried again, because she says she can hear something's wrong, and asks me to please tell her what's wrong.

I finally push the phone at Mr. Rawls, and he

convinces her to let me stay the night, saying he'll drive me back tomorrow. He winks at me as he says so, so I know he's not going to make me go back if I don't want to.

But I don't know what I want.

# 15

Mr. Rawls makes me promise not to run away again, and I spend the afternoon with Drum, cleaning the Cadillac, washing and scrubbing and waxing and polishing until everything gleams. Working helps me think, like if I'm using my energy elsewhere, my mind is more free to do its job without interference.

We don't talk anymore. Everything important has been said, but Drum keeps glancing at me, and I keep wondering how he knew I'd looked at the pills that way. I feel like he's stolen a secret from me.

When I'm not thinking about me, I'm thinking about my mom. She was very brave to run away like that. It's strange to think of my mom that way, because I always thought she wasn't brave at all, but it must have taken a lot of guts for her to run away pregnant, to go away and have me and raise me all by herself. She didn't do such a bad job, either. In lots of ways she's a great mom.

Maybe Mom isn't really sick in the head after all. Maybe it's just that the chemicals in her brain don't know what to do when stuff like that happens, because stuff like that isn't supposed to happen to people. Maybe the Nobel story was created in my mom's brain because I was about to be born and she needed to be able to love me. Maybe the only way she could keep believing the Nobel lie was if she stayed inside her own head with the science magazines and the books and her plans for my future. But when I got bigger and bigger and my Nobel genes wouldn't show themselves, she needed to escape, and that's why she started using the pills and the booze.

It is because of me that Mom is sick; it's because of me that she's lying in a coma right now.

I tell this to Drum because I need to say it out loud, and he tosses me another rag and tells me to work harder on the hubcaps. I sit down cross-legged on the floor and start cleaning, biting my lip until it hurts, and I want it to hurt.

After a while Drum comes and taps me on the

shoulder and hands me a soda. "You know," he says, and takes a swig of his beer. "Even if your mom is sick because of you, that doesn't mean it's your fault."

It makes sense. Sort of.

Evening falls. It gets dark outside the garage. Drum dries his hands on a rag and walks out into the dusk. "You've got to go now, kid," he tells me. "I promised I'd have you back around dinnertime."

"Back?"

Drum gestured toward Mr. Rawls's house. "With him. He's in charge of you now, right?"

"I guess so."

"Go!" Drum says impatiently. "I hope you'll be okay. I'll take care of the house until . . . well, as long as I'm here. Now . . . go." He turns around and retreats into the garage, and I walk over to Mr. Rawls's house, feeling Drum's eyes on me until I'm safely inside.

Mr. Rawls orders pizza for dinner and asks me if I've thought things over.

I have. Waxing the Cadillac helped me think. I know now what I want to do. We eat pizza and watch television, and then I tell Mr. Rawls that I'm ready, tell him I want to go back to my grandmother's house now, instead of in the morning.

He doesn't ask questions. Maybe because the answers don't make much sense anymore.

It's past midnight when we get back to my grandmother's house. I ask Mr. Rawls to drop me off by the gates because it's so late, so the sound of the car won't wake anybody up.

"No," he says. "You're my responsibility now. If you're going home, I have to see you all the way home." He looks at me. "If you don't want to go home, we can talk to your social worker and figure something out. Your call. But I'm not leaving you on the street."

I squirm. I don't want Grandma to greet me at the door. I want to sneak in and put my plan in action. "The door then," I say. Our father's bedroom faces the front of the house, but Grandma sleeps at the back. Maybe the car won't wake her up. "Please. Take me to the door, and you can watch me go inside. I don't want everyone to wake up. They don't expect me until morning, anyway."

Mr. Rawls drives all the way up to the darkened house without answering. He turns off the car and looks at me. "Okay. I'll drop you off here as long as I can watch you go inside. But I'll call early tomorrow morning. And I'll have to talk to your grandmother.

To make sure you're okay. That everything's okay. And when I talk to her, I want you to have talked to her first. Understand?"

"Thanks," I tell him. I pick my backpack up from the floor. "Good-bye."

Mr. Rawls squeezes my shoulder and wishes me good luck. I run toward the door, excited and afraid now that I know what to do. I use my key to enter the house, and disconnect the alarm using the code Grandma taught me. I stand on tiptoe to look out the peephole and see Mr. Rawls drive off. The car makes almost no noise, and everybody is still asleep. I sneak up the stairs and open the door into our father's bedroom.

I turn on the light and he is awake. His good eye is trying to follow me, and his hand twitches at his side. I smile at him. It feels like someone is pulling strings to make my mouth move, and it's a strange, mechanical smile. I close the door and step closer. I grab the help button, lying there close to his hand, and put it on the nightstand, out of his reach.

I think I see fear in our father's eye, and it thrills me. He can see it in my eyes; he knows that I know. I'm silent for a while; I just stand there, staring at him and letting him wonder what's going on, hoping he's suffering some of the terror and helplessness he inflicted on my mom.

I stare at him for a long time, thinking how I hate half of me because it's him—then realize it's more than that, he's half of my mother, too, so that means I'm three quarters him. I'm almost him, almost identical, like a clone.

The thought makes me nauseous again, but I look out the window and see the starry sky and remember the story of stardust drifting around the cosmos for eons and eons, and soon I'm calm again.

"I know what you are," I finally tell our father, my voice sounding hoarse and unfamiliar. Our father responds, one eye moves as if an invisible string is pulling it in random circles. "I know what you did," I say, and the gaze stops on the window, then the eyelid drops, but I know he hears me and there's nothing he can do about it. He can't leave the room, can't call for help, can't do anything but sit there and listen to what I say. The power is heady. I like it.

I don't like that I like it, because that may be his genes speaking, joy in having power over someone who's weaker. Are my genes—my painting genes—cruel and evil?

Am *I* cruel and evil?

Our father's one good eye is looking at me once again and I stare back, even though his gaze feels like it's spreading dirt all over me. I look at his IV, touch the plastic bag, and wonder if something bad would happen if it were taken away.

It would be easy. He's so weak now.

But as I stand here and hatred fills me until I tremble, I know that I'm not a killer. The ultimate revenge is not in death. My hand falls away from the IV bag and the decision feels right.

Death is easy. Life is not.

Magazines and books are piled on a table by the chair I used to sit in while I read to him. I take them and put them away in the bookshelf, neatly, so they vanish in with the other books, like I never took them out and read to him.

"You're evil," I tell him, the sound again harsh in the quiet room. "I hope you believe in God, because then you must know you're going to hell."

The eyelid flickers only slightly, and I try to think of more to say, something nasty, something mean and cruel and horrible, but it all seems pointless. So instead I turn away from him, walk to the window, and start stacking the contents of my backpack on the windowsill. I take my time, letting him wonder what I'm going to do.

"I'm going to paint a door," I tell him, and open the first paint can, my back still turned to him. They are not his paints, not paints from his studio upstairs. They're Mom's paints, from our house—every last drop remaining in the nearly empty cans I picked up from outside the door and around the house, and hid in the garage the day Mom went to the hospital. "I'm going to paint a door on the wall over here." I dip the brush in the paint can and make one long stroke on the cream-colored wall. "When you fall asleep, in your dreams, the door can open, but only from the other side. You'll dream—but it won't be your own dreams."

I don't explain anything more. I want to let him worry and wonder, assume the worst, and I get to work, his harsh breathing the only sound in the room.

I take care with this door. I make it sturdy and strong-looking, but simple. It's brown in color, as if made from old wood. I create the illusion of a lock that only opens and closes from the other side, so that he has no control over it. I leave out the hinges; they go on the other side.

When I'm finished and step back, I see that it looks just as good as my mom's first doors did. It looks almost real.

Then I pile my stuff back into my backpack and leave the room. Our father is still awake and watching, his good eye is fixed on the new door. The door won't open now, not until he falls asleep, and eventually he will.

I'm going to the hospital now, to sit with my mom and hold her hand, tell her I know everything and that it's okay. I'll try to tell her we don't need my Nobel genes anymore. I'll be me and she'll be my mom and that will be enough.

Maybe I'll fall asleep right there next to her. Maybe I will meet her in my dreams tonight, and I'll show her what I did for her; I'll show her the new door in the hallway, with the strong lock that opens only one way, for her to use any way she likes, or just keep it closed forever if she wants to. The important thing is that it's there, and that I put it there.

I don't feel dirty and wrong anymore, like I shouldn't exist. I don't have Nobel genes and I am made from question marks, thousands and thousands of question marks. Everybody is, and it's okay—I'm a riddle I'll spend my whole life solving.

My genes are not our father's, not my mom's, they're my own and they're everyone's and they're nobody's—they're not me, they're just the stuff I'm made from.

I leave the house, grab my bike from the garage, and walk it down the path toward the street. I look up at the darkened window in our father's bedroom and smile.

I bet he is afraid to fall asleep.

I mount my bike and start pedaling toward the hospital. I go as fast as I can. The chill night air rushes at me and burrows through my clothes, into my body—but I don't mind the cold now. I don't mind anything anymore.

We all come from the primordial soup, a miracle in the universe, and before that, we come from the stars.

The universe is twinkling in the sky above, and the road I take is crooked and treacherous, but it will bring me where I need to go even if I don't know the way. That's the way life works.

I'll be okay. I'm stardust.

# ACKNOWLEDGMENTS

Thank you to my agent, George Nicholson—this one was the first and I know it was always your favorite.

Thank you to my wonderful beta-readers—Pam, Kjartan, Nonni, Dúnja, and Haukur—and to CritiqueCircle.com for making the process so much easier.

This story probably set some kind of record for the number of editors who touched it along the way, but I'll restrict myself to the major players. In order of appearance: Ginee Seo, Lisa Cheng, and Namrata Tripathi—I appreciate everything each of you brought to this story.

As always, thanks to my husband, Kjartan, for your support—without you there would be no books at all.

And thank you to my little daughter, who was irresistible in all her attempts to sabotage line edits and copy edits, not to mention the laborious work on the acknowledgments. You're right, sweetie, shorter is always better, but I'll still blame you for any remaining typos. Go reticulocytes!